Readers respond to

Touchstone Season 1

"So good has got into my dreams and is only surpassed by Jack Finney, the master in time... e vein I cannot wait..."

CH0A421601

"An engaging time tr... re concentration and weavi... d back again stories."

"I ordered the whole se... and ... ...re fantastic..."

"From the first book to the last in the first season I was hooked. Some nights went to bed intending to read just a chapter or two but found myself not being able to stop reading..."

"Engrossing and never quite does what you expect..."

"Superb. Really enjoyed this series. Can't wait for more!"

Touchstone (1: The Sins of the Fathers) [1912]

"I couldn't put it down…"

"Makes for an interesting, enjoyable and easy read, and opens the reader's eyes to a time in Moseley long forgotten. It draws your attention to details of how the area was 100 years ago: the beautiful old buildings, the steam tram, how the Village green was actually green…"

"An extremely riveting short book that I didn't want to end and would have loved the book to be longer..."

"I have read a few time travel books but this one really got to me. I thought it was going to be a typical teenage romance but it certainly wasn't. Absolutely gripping…"

"I was rapt up in the story, couldn't put it down."

"I didn't expect to be so blown away as I was with this… I felt I could go and visit and really see these places. I love the characters and simply adored this book."

"Tried this out on a whim, very pleased I did, crisply written, engaging and thrilling, enjoyed it so much, I bought the series!"

"I must admit I love any books that have time travel in them, and this one didn't disappoint either. To make things even better, was to get to the end of this book knowing there were more to come. I ended up purchasing all five of the books and reading them one after the other over the space of a couple of days."

"A story to make you feel you have gone back to Birmingham in 1912. I could not put it down and can't wait to get into the next adventure."

Touchstone (2: Family at War) [1940]

"A very good short book that kept me riveted through the whole story — I never wanted it to end."

"Brings home to one what life must have been like on the Home Front, in cities suffering nightly air raids. Doesn't flinch from the true horrors of the Blitz, nor the petty squabbles amid the rubble…"

"The historical detail in these books is fantastic, found myself wanting to know more about the area and the times."

"Initially thought it purely for children, but pleasantly surprised by the author's convincing style and obvious research into the time period concerned… all in all much better than expected, will be looking out for more by this author."

"Although the Touchstone books may have been written for a younger audience, I assure you; if you are a true fan of timeslip reads these will not disappoint! Each went by far too fast and I find myself waiting in anticipation for the next instalment. Rachel and Danny, along with the characters they meet on their 'journeys' are real, likable and completely caught up in the craziness that's so drastically changed their lives. Delightfully, Andy Conway has a unique way of throwing in twists and turns when least expected. For the price, you won't be better entertained, and soon, you too will be as hooked as I am."

"Basically, it's a wonderful read - I just love these time travel books, whatever shape or form they have. This one was special… I believe it's one of the best series of its kind."

Touchstone (3: All the Time in the World) [1966]

"I've read all three of the *Touchstone* stories now and each brings the period, in this case the sixties, to life. By concentrating on one area of the world, Moseley, Andy Conway has given it a depth and realism. He turned my preconceptions of the swinging sixties upside down a couple of times."

"As per the previous two in this series, it is an interesting concept and is developing the story nicely with obviously more time eras to come with all the central characters and now this new introduction of some sort of monitoring team. Who are they? What is their function? I'll need to keep reading the series now I'm hooked."

"Enjoyable storyline giving a bit of an insight into people and life during these times. Some historical events creatively written."

"I really enjoyed Touchstone 1 and 2 so much that today while in Birmingham I went to Moseley village to see if the place were real. Thank you for writing the books…"

"Loved this one… I got so engrossed in it that I lost track of time completely (excuse the pun) and finished this in three to four days! Highly recommended to anyone who loves a good time travel tale."

Touchstone (4: Station at the End of Time) [1959]

"A cracking, spooky read with some great twists… oozes atmosphere, reminiscent of old TV shows like Sapphire and Steel or the Twilight Zone… As ever, it's a cracking read which never really stops for breath, exactly like the freight train bearing down on the protagonist's grandmother… also comes with a bonus short story which is a real head-wrecker."

"Best one yet. I really love this series of books and this is the most gripping yet. Although not familiar with Birmingham it is still fascinating to hear of the old Kings Heath station and the images it creates in my mind. Also take the time to read the short article at the end."

"This was a good read, enjoyed the whole series."

"Just read Touchstone 1-4 in one sitting. Unfortunately, I have now time-travelled up to your writing speed. Looking forward to Touchstone 5."

Touchstone (5: Let's Fall in Love for the Last Time) [1934]

"I've thoroughly enjoyed every bit of this series… this is an incredible story. If, like me, you love time travel novels, you'll love this."

"The plot is definitely thickening. Over the course of the five books, with the brilliant slight diversion of book 4, I have fallen deeper and deeper into the story of Rachel and Danny and the stories of the people around them."

"I am by far a *huge* fan of anything time travel related, and this series of time travel books had me hooked from book number one."

"What a find! I have never read anything by Andy Conway before — but I'm now hooked! Not only was the story thoroughly enjoyable, it was also very thought provoking. Andy Conway certainly makes you think about how ordinary people lived and how their values and belief systems have changed so dramatically over the past 100 years."

"Waited, waited, waited and waited for this. Now read it. Loved it. Can't wait for the next one. Also looking forward to the spin off sequels. Amazing story."

Touchstone (6: Fade to Grey) [1980]

"This series has had me hooked from start to finish. I'm sad it's ended but glad it's not the end. I'm now looking forward to the next season. It's a magnificent story."

"A great series and a fine final episode, probably the best yet and by far the longest. Can't wait for series two, I am going to miss going to bed with this book at night!"

"Absolutely Superb! I have thoroughly enjoyed the whole *Touchstone* series and I have to say I've been eagerly awaiting this one, the last in the series. I wasn't disappointed in any way! If you haven't read this series yet — you simply must! Go and download *Touchstone 1. The Sins of the Fathers* — but beware — you will be hooked!!"

Buried in Time [1888]

"Inventively brilliant alternative history. Enjoyed the first Touchstone series and this is deeper, darker and more inventive."

"Everyone loves a good Jack the Ripper tale. This is one."

"A brilliant book again from Andy Conway."

"Very good."

"Cracking read."

"Great read, and thought provoking on whom Jack the Ripper really was. Look forward to reading series 2."

"Another riveting read. Another excellent book from Andy Conway."

Bright Star Falling [1874-87]

"I have been waiting for the release of the eighth novel in the Touchstone series and this fabulous book definitely did not disappoint. It immerses the reader in the fascinating and tragic world of the Native Americans whilst still keeping the Touchstone theme. A brilliant and enjoyable read, I couldn't put it down!"

"Fantastic story . A world away from the Birmingham of season one but the Wild West and time travel what a brilliant combination."

"We had to wait a while for the next instalment in the Touchstone series. But it was well worth waiting for."

"As a huge fan of time-travel fiction and film I devoured the first Touchstone series, and Season Two has certainly got off on the right footing. From Jack the Ripper to the Wild West via a hipster Birmingham suburb… I love the way the series is so close to home, whilst effortlessly dancing over centuries – and the globe… with truly educational and sensitive depictions of the Lakota, and the events and skirmishes leading up to what is known as "Custer's Last Stand"… it's a great book."

"A good read. One gets the impression that the author has done his historical homework, so one really seems to get a 'feel' of the time and so learns something in addition to being well entertained."

"Well written and immersive with a real sense of place and time. You feel that the author has really done his research. Great storytelling as always, can't wait for the next one."

Bright Star Rising [1887]

"Touchstone saga at its best. Absolutely brilliant and highly recommended."

"Another brilliant book in the Touchstone series. The story twists and turns, with so much detail and strong links to Birmingham in another time."

Andy Conway is the novelist, screenwriter and time traveller behind the Touchstone series. He wrote the feature films *Arjun & Alison*, *An American Exorcism* and *The Courier* and runs a publishing empire from a loft in Birmingham.

Read more at andyconway.net

Photography: Ian Davies iandaviesphoto.com

THE GHOSTS OF PARADISE PLACE

WALLBANK

This paperback edition 2019
1

First published in Great Britain by
Wallbank Books 2019
Copyright © Andy Conway 2019
The right of Andy Conway to be identified as the author of this
work has been asserted by him in accordance with the Copyright,
Designs and Patent Act, 1988 © Andy Conway 2019

ISBN-9781087498379

Cover design by Sean Strong
www.seanstrong.com

To Danny, Steph and Ellie.
True friends and fans.

— 1 —

It began with a dream that wasn't a dream. The kind so vivid you woke with skin clammy from running, only just escaping through the gate between the world of sleep and reality, a hand snatching at your hair, to wake gasping, wondering whose hand it was that snatched at you, who it was that chased you into morning.

In the dream that wasn't a dream, she saw herself, as if outside herself, as if seeing herself through another's eyes.

A woman at night in a whirling snowstorm, a shawl that barely covered her bright red hair, a stone tower behind her, whipped by waves of angry snow churning the night sky.

She turned, eyes flashing dark fire, and for a moment felt terror at her own look.

And then she was running past the Parthenon columns of the Town Hall in the centre of Birmingham.

Dark figures in the street, raggedy children in putrid gutters, men in top hats and flat caps and women in bonnets. Snow, deep and crisp and evil.

A Dickensian Christmas card turned nightmare.

She caught a flash of a poster on the side of the Town

Hall as she ran, proclaiming a reading by Charles Dickens, as if to confirm her dream.

She ran on down the gaslit street, dark figures chasing her, the pant of their dog breath on her neck, their boots slapping snow and mud.

An old lady stepped out into the street holding out a hand to stop her. A kind face, warm grey eyes. "Katherine! Katherine, my dear!" she cried. "Wait! Stop!"

Kath bundled on, hurtling into snowblind fog, skin clammy from running, and just as a hand grabbed at her hair, she woke.

— 2 —

Lying awake, she was aware of the dark before she was aware of herself. A new day, sullen and freezing beyond the curtains.

The cold she had to face. An intense desire to stay curled up under the warm duvet. She stretched out her leg to the other half of the bed, the empty half of the bed, and felt the sheets cold. She drew her foot back into the heat of her cocoon.

Why had she taken the bed? She might have left it there with him. Because it was expensive. Relocating had been expensive enough without having to buy a new bed. But it just reminded her of him and his absence.

She had broken up with Darren four weeks ago, had moved out of their house in Selly Oak, and was renting this ground floor flat on the edge of Moseley.

The bed was almost the only piece of furniture she possessed. If she hadn't claimed it, this place would be empty.

More galling was the box of his stuff she'd accidentally taken with her. A few weeks of sullen arguments by text message had followed, Darren making idiotic accusations. How dare she take his stuff? How dare she give him the hassle of coming a mile to collect it from her? It was almost as if she couldn't let go and wanted to see him again, he wrote.

She'd had to rummage through it and list what was in it. And now he didn't want it anymore. He was happy to let it go, desperate not to see her again.

She eased her head up and leaned on one elbow, tucking her red hair behind her ears, clutching the duvet around her, unwilling to let the heat escape.

She should burn it. Burn it in the garden. It would be cleansing. Perhaps before Christmas. Burn his box full of crap in the back garden like some pagan winter solstice ghost-banishing rite.

No, she thought, that just sounded crazy. Loneliness was turning her into a demented old witch.

She swung her legs off the bed, her bare feet cringing at the cold floor.

A new day, a new job. Christmas on the horizon. It was time to banish him and any thoughts of loneliness. If you allowed yourself to dwell on the past, it would consume you in its cloud of depression. You had to forget it all and look forward. *Never look back or the devil will get you.*

She shrugged off the duvet and rushed across bare floorboards to the bathroom, and in moments was gasping naked under hot spray.

— 3 —

Leaving her ground floor flat, the door clattered shut, echoing back in the emptiness. She crossed the street, thick with rush hour traffic almost at a standstill, and walked down the hill to the bus stop on the other side.

A cluster of sullen adults waiting for the next 50 bus into town, a couple of them at the front of the shelter chatting politely. Would these faces become familiar in time, the group that all caught the bus to work at about this time of morning?

The school behind the bank of trees was already swarming like a hive, the chaos of kids congregating. Insane chatter. Perhaps they were breaking up soon for Christmas, lessons replaced by concerts, games, crafts. She remembered her whole school watching films projected in the assembly hall for end of term and wondered if they still did that.

The bus came, she showed her pass to the driver and went upstairs, finding a seat alone. The bus eased up the hill in the line of traffic, so slow, and she laughed to herself when it passed her house after a couple of minutes. She could have walked the other way down to Moseley and perhaps caught a 50 that was stuck in traffic there.

She viewed her new house, a third of a house, assessing it from above and afar, as if she was a stranger passing by. A down-at-heel row of mock Tudor three-storey houses divided into flats. She now lived in that strip of road between Moseley and Kings Heath, which seemed to be neither here nor there. In times past, maybe there hadn't even been any dwellings here at all. There would have been a cluster of houses around St Mary's church in Moseley, and another cluster around All Saints in Kings Heath, and this would have been a dirt track between the two, a dirt track over the hill that hid one village from the other.

She would have to dig out the old Ordnance Survey maps at the Library to see if that's what it was like. At some point, it must have been. You just had to go back far enough in time.

She smiled and wondered if she'd ever have time for that, working right there in the place where she'd always researched for the fun of it. If it was your job, maybe you never did it for pleasure again.

The bus crested the hill and snaked down to Moseley village.

A whisper at her shoulder.

She flinched and turned, expecting a passenger behind her. Had someone tapped her on the shoulder?

No. The seat behind was empty.

Outside, a stone tower in the grounds of Moseley Hall Hospital.

The dovecote.

She shuddered. Something about it. A haunting presence. Brooding.

It was a quaint little tower, an urban folly. So why

did it feel like a gargoyle on a church glowering down at respectable people in their Sunday best, an ugly threat from a dark past?

She shut it out as the bus sailed on down through Moseley village and headed for the city.

She walked through the city centre, the 2008 German Christmas Market stalls all the way up New Street opening for *glühwein* and beer. Christmas lights obscuring the view of the Parthenon-style pillars of the old Town Hall building.

There was talk of the German market being a failure this year, because of the credit crunch. Banks failing everywhere. But it seemed that everything carried on as normal. People still went to work and got paid and spent their money on Christmas.

In her handbag she'd packed a peanut butter sandwich. The jar would last till New Year so she wouldn't have to buy lunch. The bus pass she'd bought would cover her. She had enough money to last till Christmas and they'd promised to give her an advance on her end of month pay. Three weeks of lean times, but she could manage.

She turned into Victoria Square, so crowded with wooden shacks selling beer and bratwurst that its usual decorations seemed lost. The giant *Iron:Man* sculpture that stood before the Council House, at a tilt, as if about to fall over, the steps leading up to and around a tumbling fountain, the enormous goddess lying in the fountain at the top of the steps. *The Floozie in the Jacuzzi,* they called it. A goddess reduced to a stupid joke. Stone gryphon figures guarded the square. She skipped up the steps past the fountain and the carousel, through the gap where the corner of the Town Hall almost touched the corner of the Council House.

Chamberlain Square hiding behind it. An amphitheatre of concrete steps with old statues of city fathers looking down on the ornate Victorian fountain at the centre, and the Brutalist inverted ziggurat of the Birmingham Central Library ringing the square.

She paused and took it in. She'd spent her youth here, had dreamed of working here, and now she was starting her first day.

It didn't seem like the culmination of a childhood dream.

It was just the break-up. A dead relationship was like a dead relative: it haunted you. You had to shake off the ghosts and move forward.

She walked to the glass doors and waved to the security guard who was letting staff in.

"Morning," she said. "I'm Katherine Bright. It's my first day."

He checked his list and waved her through the electronic security gate, for the first time as an employee, not a girl just coming to research and hide from the world among the six floors of silent stacks.

She took the escalators up to the sixth instead of the lift, because it was more pleasant to pass through each orange-carpeted floor and see the vast acres all empty, just a handful of staff setting up for the day.

A librarian, she thought. *I'm a librarian now.*

She suppressed a manic giggle fizzing in her throat at the thought of tying her red hair up in a tight bun and wearing glasses to live the cliché.

The smile was still all bright on her face as she reached the Local Studies department on the sixth floor, so she squinted to look more serious.

At the Local Studies reception desk, a man in a tweed jacket and bow tie looked up. "Katherine, welcome. Do come round."

This was the moment she would get to see the other side. It thrilled her more than it should. She lifted the flap in the white Formica counter and stepped through to his handshake.

Too firm, just like at the interview. Timothy. A posh boy. Ruddy complexion. He might be her father's age, she thought, but his voice sounded younger. She couldn't work it out.

He showed her through to a pokey staff room behind the counter, with a sofa and a kettle in one corner, crowded by shelving and box files. Once she'd deposited her coat and handbag, Timothy led her through to the wide-open space of the stacks to an exhibition area, screened off.

"Might as well show you this right away. This is where Liz is preparing the next exhibition, which opens Saturday."

They squeezed through a gap in the hessian screens to a wide oblong of about thirty feet long. A block of wooden chairs laid out in the middle ready for a talk. In giant lettering, old-fashioned like the old BBC logo, were the words *Brave New City,* each letter in a slanted box with rounded corners.

"All our exhibitions are focussed around talks and

events now. Outreach and such. We need to get people in here, and that means putting on events. They really love a bit of local history. Nice, cosy stories about the past."

Giant photographs of the city from the 1960s lined the exhibition space, and Katherine thrilled at the sight of streets she knew transformed through the filter of the past.

"Liz put this one together. You'll meet her in a minute. I think of this as our Swinging Sixties event."

"It's my favourite era, the Sixties," Katherine said. "You know, the styles and the music."

"Excellent. That's the idea. To appeal to young people like us. Get them in here. Of course, we have to do Victorian stuff for the old ones too."

So he was the same age as her. Late twenties. It was just that he dressed like her granddad and had the easy charm of a boy who'd always been told the world owed him a living.

She strolled along the presentation panels. An interesting collection of photographs, all muted orange-browns and clean lines, much like the Central Library.

"It's a great find," Timothy said. "An amazing collection that's been in an archive for years. Lovely stuff. And she really captures that essence of life during the Swinging Sixties, when the city had an ultra-modern makeover and shook off its old Victorian overcoat. Birmingham was such a go-ahead city then. They built the Rotunda, this library, the Bull Ring shopping centre. All modern and sleek."

Kath bent down and peered at a curious photograph. A bunch of people posing. At the centre a man who was clearly the mayor, wearing his ceremonial chain,

13

surrounded by a bunch of sharp-suited men, old and young, and girls who'd walked right off Carnaby Street, holding trays of drinks. Models hired to be waitresses.

A young man caught her eye, staring out with a gaze that seemed to reach out and grab her. A shiver of *déjà vu.* Had she seen him before? Was he a film star or something?

The panel of text beside it said: *World Cup 1966, Villa Park. The mayor with town planners at the West Germany vs Spain group game.*

"Of course, they're knocking all that stuff down now," Timothy droned. "All those underpasses rather made the city a place for cars, not people. And those ghastly blocks of flats."

He paused, as if drifting off to an uncomfortable memory he couldn't quite reconcile with this moment. Then he clapped his hands, as if to shoo it away.

Kath blinked and tore her eyes away from the photograph and the haunting gaze of the man within it.

"But we're going to concentrate on the positive stuff. It's all about giving them history in a cosy way. Minis and mini-skirts; that's what the public want. For the next exhibition, you've got to find the Victorian equivalent to that."

He took her back behind the reception counter, where a blonde woman was setting up. Katherine recognized her from years of using the library, and now she would be her workmate. She was maybe a few years older than Kath, possibly thirty. No make-up at all, just a natural, haunting beauty, and Kath remembered how she'd always found her a bit scary, as if she wasn't quite of this world, serene and detached, like a Botticelli angel. Kath had always felt she wasn't worthy enough to be

14

bothering this woman with queries. She couldn't remember if she'd ever talked to her at all.

"This is Liz. I'll leave you in her capable hands." He went off and left them alone.

Liz shook her hand, her fingers cool and white, like porcelain. "Hello, Katherine. Did he give you the cosy past speech?"

"Er, yes he did."

"He gave me that too. It's a load of tosh. The past isn't nice and cosy. It's mean and brutal."

"How do you know?" Katherine shrugged and grinned, making it clear she was joking, not challenging her.

Liz smirked, and it was the first time Kath had ever seen anything remotely like a smile on her face. "I don't. But my mum always told me the Swinging Sixties weren't quite so glamorous when you knew everyone had an outside loo. It looks lovely on the photographs, but can you imagine what Birmingham used to smell like?"

"Yes, I suppose."

"But anyway, welcome to Local Studies. Let me show you where everything is and get you on this archaic computer system of ours."

— 5 —

Her first week of work went by and she settled into the place like a new pair of shoes. It was mostly handling research requests from the public: *the Greys*, Liz called them, as they all seemed to be retired. They came and took up the desk spaces all day and pored through the volumes of old city directories, the microfiches of births and deaths, wills, war records, council records. You could piece together every moment of the city's history if you had a mind to.

The sixth floor was not in fact the top floor. A spiral staircase in the middle of Local Studies led to an upper research room that was smaller, cosier. She preferred working in this room, luxuriating in the pregnant quiet. It felt remote from the rest of the building. An ivory tower.

While not dealing with general duties and getting up to speed on how the library system worked, she tried to find time to prepare her first exhibition that would launch in the New Year.

Timothy came up to the seventh floor and hovered around, pretending to be sorting stuff out in the storeroom just off the seventh floor counter.

Kath felt him nearby, the way you know someone is taking you in, behind your back.

She felt his presence, too close. He leaned over her shoulder, his hand on the counter next to hers. She drew her hand away and hid it on her lap.

'How's it going with the next exhibition? I trust Saturday gave you lots of inspiration?'

He chortled. Actually *chortled*. It was the only word for it.

"I'm a little stuck to be honest," she said.

"It's a simple historical exhibition about some nice things at Moseley Hall. Nice and cosy."

Kath felt a sudden urgent need to dodge out of his cloud of aftershave.

"It's a hospital now, of course," he said. "But it was part of the Cadbury estate, and before that Joseph Priestley's manor house. So much history."

"Perhaps too much. Difficult to find an angle."

"You know," he said, "there's a really fascinating piece of film in the archives. You absolutely have to have it as the centrepiece of the exhibition. It's from the 1930s and it shows a gymkhana tournament in the grounds. A beautiful, idyllic British summer. The absolute picture of Home and Empire. You must track it down. Huntley Archive."

He took a step back and Kath breathed, scribbling down his suggestion to busy her hands.

"Huntley Archive. Thank you."

"Very good," he said, and tootled off down the spiral staircase, whistling something tuneless.

She looked up the reference and went through to the stacks to find it, but it was missing.

Someone must have taken it out, she thought, and

made a note to trace it.

Back at her desk, she leafed through the pile of photographs she'd collected and paused at a picture of the Dovecote.

A whisper at her shoulder.

That feeling again. A ghost behind her.

She shuddered it away like a dog shaking off the rain, and looked around the research room. A handful of Greys quietly browsing through archives.

A man in a waistcoat, his white shirtsleeves rolled up, walked through the door marked *Staff Only* at the other end.

Kath stood. Had that been a member of the public?

She strode over and pushed through.

Beyond the door were acres of shelves that the public never saw. Over two-thirds of the gigantic inverted ziggurat was a vast warehouse of reference books and files.

"Excuse me," she said. Too quiet.

The man ignored her and kept on walking. His confidence made her doubt herself. It was as if he had a right to be there, to walk wherever he liked. Perhaps he was a manager she hadn't met yet.

Footsteps echoing. He dodged into the stacks.

She rushed after.

He was gone.

She couldn't hear his footsteps any longer. Perhaps he'd gone through to the other side of the building. He must have been a member of staff or he wouldn't have walked on so boldly.

She went back to the research room and resumed her studies into Moseley Hall. The picture of the dovecote that had spooked her, lying there on her desk.

— 6 —

As the afternoon waned, she found herself delving into a fascinating story of a witch trial in Birmingham in the 1700s. Selly Oak had allegedly been named after a witch who'd been hanged and buried at a crossroads with an oak stake through her heart. The oak had grown into a tree. *Sally's Oak.* A notorious Puritan clergyman and witch-finder, Edmund Meckle, had passed through the hamlet and put her on trial. There were no historical records for any of it; just whispers and rumours that had floated down the centuries. A folk tale. A warning to women not to step out of line.

Three hours later the library was closing. She had fallen through a rabbit hole of research and forgotten all time.

Liz was gone. It was Friday night.

Katherine closed up and left the building, rushing head down through the crowds thronging the German market, hordes of suited workers necking Hofbrau and *glühwein.*

She got a 50 bus home to her Spartan ground floor flat and opened the tiny freezer compartment of the fridge. A stack of ready-made meals in tiny foil trays, marked *For One Person.* She microwaved a macaroni cheese and ate it sullenly before TV news. DNA analysis had identified human remains found in Russia in 1991 as Tsar Nicholas. She gawped at history and science meeting. She was almost a scientist herself, patiently uncovering the physical artefacts of the past, even if those artefacts were only words and images kept in dusty archives.

At nine, she looked around at the depressing reality of her life. A lone woman of nearly thirty in an empty flat on a Friday night, with no friends and no social life.

She had had friends. But when she'd split with Darren she'd found they were all his friends, not hers.

She slapped on some make-up and changed into a lovely blue Mary Quant dress she'd bought at a vintage fair, with a 60s coat, too thin for winter. It was freezing, but only a short trip to Moseley. She hopped on the 50. It was a handful of stops and she could have walked there in five minutes, but the bus was warm.

She stepped off in the village and took it in. This was Moseley. You *had* to go to the Prince of Wales for a drink on Friday night.

Entering a bar alone. Her mum had told her that was never the done thing. A woman alone in a bar. That meant you were a tart. It didn't matter. Things were different now. It was 2008. Katherine could walk into any bar she chose and order what she liked, and no one would give her so much as a sideways glance. She had a feeling it was doubly so here in Moseley.

Besides, she was here in a new place with no bloody friends. She was desperate.

She ordered a dry white wine, small, and thought she could neck it and go home if it was all too much.

A stool at the bar was free so she took it, next to a bunch of old blokes in a circle. She took out her iPhone and scrolled through Faceparty for a while, thinking everyone in the bar must be watching, judging. The iPhone had been an absurd indulgence before the split with Darren, and now she had no money it made her sick to own it.

She could see clear through to the corridor at the back, through the rear hatch where drinkers lined up to be served. There were two cosy rooms off to each side and the beer garden at the rear.

An awful thought. She might see her Darren. What if he was here with his mates, or even worse, with a new girl?

A familiar face at the hatch opposite. A double take. It was Liz. She nodded a greeting, like a man would with a vague acquaintance.

Kath waved and then shoved her hand under the bar.

Liz ordered drinks, three glasses of wine and retreated to the room on the left.

Kath checked the inch of white wine left in her own glass and wondered how long she could make it last. Should she order another and go try to join Liz, make a connection, or just knock it back and leave?

She scrolled through MySpace, looking at the interesting lives of people she barely knew, sipping at her wine till it was almost gone. Should she have brought a book with her, or would that look even worse? You could read a book on your phone now, apparently. Ebooks, they called them.

"You waiting for someone?"

At her shoulder. It was Liz.

"No. Just having a quiet drink."

"That's brave. Come and sit with us, if you like."

She walked off and left it like that. Kath looked around the front bar. No one had noticed. She ordered another small white wine, stepped off the high stool and walked round to the rear corridor.

Liz was sitting in the room to the left, which been done out to resemble a Victorian reading room. She had two girlfriends, Sian and Zara, and they were talking excitedly about their imminent Christmas trip to Dartmoor. They'd booked a cottage and were going to spend Christmas away from everything.

"Away from men," Sian said.

Kath detected the sad bravado of a woman who'd been dumped. She listened to their plans and smiled politely, shifting on her stool as if trying to adjust to the collision of work and private life.

Sian got up to get a round and Zara went to help her. Kath declined, and showed her full glass. It was vitally important to avoid getting into a round with three women who drank wine by the bucket.

Liz gazed into the distance for a few moments then opened her mouth to speak. "There's something…" She shook her head and shrugged it away.

There was something about the forthcoming trip that was unnerving her, Kath could tell, some secret between them all. Or maybe she was just dreading being with these two close friends for Christmas.

"I found something really interesting for the next exhibition," Kath said, and wondered why she'd brought it back to work at the first opportunity.

Because that was all they had in common.

"Oh yes?" Liz asked.

"A news story about a murder trial. There was a series

of witch sightings around the dovecote in 1889. A strange looking woman appearing at night. Then fingers were pointed at a local woman. But as they no longer burned witches, she was safe. Apparently. Till some local man decided to murder her because she'd ruined his business."

"Gruesome."

"I was thinking of tying it in to the witch hunts of a hundred years earlier. You know that Selly Oak got its name from *Sally's Oak*, where they hanged a witch?"

"Timothy won't let you feature that," Liz said. "Too dark."

"But it's interesting."

"The cosy past, remember. In fact, he's just policing our view of the past. He won't want it because it reveals all the uncomfortable facts about how women were treated, and we can't have that."

Kath saw all her research and the fire in her heart it had engendered, circling the plughole. A wasted day. "You don't think he'll let me use it?"

"No. But it's what we should be telling people about: the stupid brutality of their bloody ancestors."

Sian and Zara came back, and the talk turned to Dartmoor again. They even took out a map and discussed a long walk across the moor they had planned. Kath found herself thinking how nice it would be to do that. But not with three women.

The evening blurred; she learned that Sian had recently divorced, and they all hated her stupid husband, Ian. She might have even told them about her own break up with stupid Darren. She wasn't sure.

As she went to leave, Liz pulled her into a hug.

Kath squirmed, embarrassed at her drunken affection.

But no. Liz hissed in her ear. "You should know Timothy wants you to fail your probation period. He wants his friend in the job and he's furious they gave it to you. He's going to make sure you fail."

"What do you mean?"

But Liz sat down with a bump and knocked her wine glass over.

Kath scurried out, head swimming, and stomped through the lively, crowded village, up the dark hill, not feeling the cold at all.

A whisper.

The dovecote across the street. Something sinister about it. A brooding presence. It buzzed with an electric power that resonated in her breastbone, as if it were a power station and she could feel its vibration humming through her.

But there was a power station next door. Or a telephone exchange. It wasn't clear. A flat-faced plastic-panelled 1960s building set back from the road. Perhaps it was that. Perhaps she was hypersensitive and could feel electricity now. Her boyfriend's jokes about her being a crazy redhead came back to her. *Ex*-boyfriend. All said in jest, though once, near the end, said with real venom.

Screw him, she thought. She'd show him.

And as she walked on over the hill, she wasn't sure if she was thinking about her ex or her boss.

— 7 —

Head throbbing and her stomach lurching, she staggered into work, fighting back the retching urge as she passed the German beer stalls opening for the Saturday. The library would open at ten. It was Liz's *Brave New City* exhibition opening, so everyone had to work the day. Kath didn't mind. It was the only chance she would get to see up close how to launch her own exhibition; see how the job was actually done.

Why had she got so drunk last night? Why had Liz, for that matter?

She stumbled through the security barriers, a tight smile to the guys on the door, hoping she wouldn't vomit on their shoes, and headed for the elevator hidden down the corridor beyond the children's library, its glass frontage festooned with a tacked-up paper mural. Some art project that looked like a great Jackson Pollock painting and made her head swirl.

The elevator lurched and shuddered up to the sixth floor and she stepped out to the glare of fluorescent strip light bouncing off acres of orange carpet.

A team of Facilities men in City Council polo shirts were taking down the big hessian covered room divider panels to reveal the new exhibition.

Liz was supervising them, a clipboard tucked under her arm. Kath went over to say hello, still in her coat.

"Morning," said Liz.

Kath looked over her shoulder, checking to see if Timothy was around. "About that thing you said last n—"

"You know, you sort of look the part," Liz said. "Very sixties."

Kath shrugged. She hadn't intended to, but perhaps unconsciously had dressed a little more retro.

Liz wasn't going to refer to it: the thing she'd said about Timothy. Had it been drunken rambling?

They strolled around the exhibition space, imagining how the public would see it.

"It looks great," Kath said.

"You know, we were talking about how Timothy sanitises it all last night?" Liz said, looking over her shoulder. "Well, there's actually a story he vetoed for this."

Liz reached under her clipboard and opened a card folder, pulling out a single sheet of paper. A photocopy of a news story.

Dark 'mob' scandal that shames our city.

Kath scanned the content as Liz talked.

"I found some really juicy stories in the news archives about a local gangster who built up a construction empire by giving bribes to councillors. They concreted this city on dodgy deals like that. Never mind Tsar Nicholas, they could run some DNA tests on the foundations of the Spaghetti Junction. You'd find a few missing persons who got in Bernie Powell's way."

Kath felt the hope for her witch story fading. If

Timothy wouldn't let this in, Kath's grubby Victorian murder story had no chance. "This reminds me of something interesting I saw. In this photo over here."

She led Liz to the World Cup photograph. The mayor surrounded by councillors and pretty girls.

Kath pointed to the mysterious young man in the group. "Who's that man? I recognize him."

Liz peered closer and shrugged. "No idea."

"He looks really familiar, like I've seen him before. I thought he might be a film star or something. Maybe a footballer?"

"No one I know. Just a council hanger-on probably."

Kath shivered and swallowed acid reflux.

"Are you okay?"

"Not really. I'm a bit rough this morning, actually."

Liz smirked and elbowed her in the ribs. "Can't take your drink."

"I really can't."

"Go out for a *glühwein* at lunch. Hair of the dog. Better still, go and get one now. I'll cover for you."

Kath shuddered and shook her head. "No. I'd just die. Besides." She checked her wristwatch. "It's opening time."

She doffed her coat and handbag, and got to work, wondering if she'd make it through to five without throwing up in Liz's exhibition.

The guest speakers arrived and Liz ran through the schedule with them. The place started to fill up and people took seats for the talk.

She had expected the audience to be the older crowd, *the Greys,* the white-haired boomers who were always up here on the sixth floor, but there were only a few of them. It was mostly younger people in their thirties and forties, a few in full Mod regalia who looked like time travellers walking in from the past. Kath recognized them from a Mod night she'd gone to a few times. For one evening every month, the upstairs room of a pub was turned into a nightclub from 1966, or how they imagined a nightclub in 1966 might look. Everyone would turn up in their Mod clothes and shimmy to beats from the Hit Parade. It was tacky and false, but at the edges of the room she had divined something that thrilled her — the feeling that she might slip into the past. However, it was the sort of time travel that took you to a place where everyone dressed like they might be in the past but they all had mobile phones.

Darren had loved it. Kath wondered if he were taking some other girl to it now.

He wouldn't come here today for this exhibition, would he?

Her belly flipped and she reached out and gripped the edge of a bookcase, anchoring herself. The thought of him walking in here with a new girlfriend. She really would be sick on his shoes.

But he would come and see the exhibition, at some point, that was certain. She would no doubt bump into him.

Just before the talk commenced, Liz left the speakers with Timothy, who would take over and pretend he'd organised the whole thing. She came to Kath's side.

"Forty-eight," said Kath. "I've counted them."

"And a young crowd. Timothy will be so pleased. God knows why they've come."

"It's interesting."

"But it's not their past. None of this lot can remember any of this. Same with the older lot."

"They only come for the Victorian stuff?"

"Oh yes," said Liz. "They can't get enough of that. *This* is their past, but the Victorian stuff is their parents' time, their grandparents'."

"I guess everyone wants a past that's just out of reach."

Timothy came over with the guest speakers. He was surely going to introduce them to Liz, who'd organised the whole thing, but he simply muttered, "Kath, see how good this exhibition is… yours will have to be better."

He led the speakers to their seats and launched into a long introduction. How proud he was to present this startling exhibition of lost photographs, how proud he was to welcome them all to the Birmingham Central Library, how pleased he was.

Liz betrayed no anger. She watched in a docile fog, as if in a trance. As if this happened all the time.

The guest speakers talked passionately about the photo collection and how it needed to be on permanent exhibition, and one of them related how it had almost been thrown out, practically rescued from a skip.

A gasp of outrage from the audience.

"Our city doesn't respect its past. It rather chooses to bulldoze it and build something new."

Applause.

When the talk was over and the audience dispersed to view the exhibition, Kath turned to Liz and was about to say, *Congratulations, you must be so proud.*

But Liz said, "I can't wait for Christmas. Three weeks away from this dump." She must have caught Kath startled look because she added, "I'm not a great advert for you in your new job, am I?"

"It's fine. We all get stressed about things."

"I wouldn't get too comfy here," said Liz.

Was this her acknowledging what she'd said last night? But Liz just shrugged and it was clear she didn't mean that at all — just that the job was awful and they were all best off out of it.

Kath felt the familiar rise of nausea in her belly and excused herself.

She took the elevator down to the second floor and the toilets at the bottom of the escalators, rushing inside a cubicle, thinking she would throw up. But nothing came. She went to the sinks and splashed cold water on her face, breathing hard. This was going to be a rough day.

As she came out of the toilets, she paused at the foot of the escalators and looked down through the giant windows on the central atrium, the shops and bars below. The stream of people walking through.

In a month or more, after Christmas, it would be her going through this.

Except it wouldn't. There was no way Timothy was going to let that happen.

— 8 —

When the talk was over, they took the chairs away and it became a simple open exhibition space. The floor returned to normal and it was just a Saturday afternoon in Local Studies. The light through the windows began to wane, winter afternoon, the faint hubbub from the German market drifting up, as the city transitioned from a Christmas shopping day to a night of revelry.

Kath busied herself up in the cosy research room on the seventh floor. A great pile of photographs had to be taken back to the reference stacks not open to the public. Kath flicked through them and stopped at an old picture.

Native Americans riding down New Street.

On the corner, just in front of the old Cornish Brothers bookshop, a bundle of Peaky Blinders gazing up at them in wonder. A gentleman with a Gladstone bag. A smart young man in a straw boater.

That whisper at her shoulder again.

Déjà vu. She had seen this before.

She flipped the photograph over and read a printed label. *Sioux Indians parade on New Street as Buffalo Bill's Wild West show visits Birmingham. November third, 1887.*

She stared at the photograph for five minutes, haunted, amazed to discover this could have happened on the street just outside and that at the same time she had always known it.

She packed it away and carried the box file through the door marked *Staff Only,* checking the catalogue number to find the shelf.

There appeared to be a gap.

Between the stacks, she found a door open. A dim green light seeped through from the other side.

She pushed the door with her foot, and let out a surprised *oh.*

A Victorian reading room, much like the Shakespeare Room they had preserved in the Conservatoire next door, its quaint, ornate style totally at odds with the Brutalist architecture of the library.

There were shelves lined with leather-bound volumes, and eerie green pools of light from banker's lamps on leather-inlaid desks.

A shuffle. The sense of another being.

She turned to see a man at the desk, his face lit by the eerie green glow. A man in a suit with a starched white collar and bow tie. She thought it was Timothy at first, but this man had a moustache, the tips waxed up into points.

"Oh," she said. "I didn't know."

She wasn't sure what it was she didn't know and why she had said that.

The man stared.

She retreated and went back out to the stacks.

There. There was the shelf she needed. How had she missed it? She shoved the box file in the correct place and hurried back through to the public space of the seventh floor research room.

She wasn't sure why she was palpitating, why the meeting had affected her so, and why she had fled to this room that felt safe. Grey haired men and women hunched over old documents. One of them looked up from his work. An old man in a fleece and stone-washed jeans. As if he'd asked her a question and was waiting for an answer.

She rushed on past and skittered down the spiral staircase to the sixth floor.

"Are you all right?" Liz asked.

She nodded and smiled it away. "I had a spooky turn. That old room upstairs. The one that's like the Shakespeare Room. I didn't know it was there."

"What old room?"

She could see from Liz's face this wasn't a joke. Kath shook her head and laughed. "Nothing. The reference stacks. They just spooked me out."

Liz wheedled about how the reference stacks were so vast and empty and she didn't like to be there once the sun went down, which was late afternoon at this time of year.

The half-hour-to-closing warning went out over the tannoy all over the building. Liz told her to go upstairs and round up everyone in the research room.

Kath went back up the spiral stairs and walked around every person at the research desks, telling each one they had to pack up.

She went back to the door to the research stacks, pushed through and crept along the shelves.

She came to that space where she'd seen the open door with the green glow.

There was no door.
It was just a blank concrete wall.

— 9 —

They closed up and Kath wondered if she would have to head back to Moseley with Liz and make awkward conversation on the bus. She wanted to be alone. But Liz said she was meeting her friends in town for a drink at the German market, so Kath grabbed her things and left, relieved.

The bus trip home was crowded with shoppers, the windows steamed up, the air musty. She closed her eyes and imagined the route from the twists and turns of the bus, the way it rose and dipped. When she thought they were just leaving Balsall Heath, by the Moseley Dance Centre, she wiped the window with her gloved hand. They had already gone through Moseley village and were climbing the hill, passing the dovecote.

A Victorian reading room right there in the middle of the concrete modernist library. And it didn't exist.

But it had been there. She was sure it had been there.

She had seen it.

Had she seen it? Could it have been a delusion? Could she be seeing things? She had always heard the phrase *seeing things* and never thought that it could mean seeing something with such clarity: seeing it, hearing it, smelling it. There had been a distinct smell about the room, of wax polish and perhaps the leather of the volumes. Above all, she had felt it. Felt it in every pore.

She got off the bus and wondered if she should go to the doctor. Saturday afternoon, almost Saturday night. There was no way she would get an appointment. The doctor's surgery would be closed anyhow. Did they even open at the weekend?

No, the only thing she could do was walk into a hospital and say, "Help me, I think I might be crazy."

You could do that, surely? You could walk into a hospital and say you needed to be sectioned. People probably did it all the time. Mad people.

She could say, "I'm seeing things that aren't there. Surely that makes me mad?"

She stumbled into her ground floor flat, turned up the heating, desperately trying to warm the place up, and made a cup of Earl Grey. She sipped it standing in the kitchen, leaning against the worktop in her coat and beret.

She rifled through the medicine cabinet in the bathroom for anything that might help her. The only thing she had was some Xanax. She took a couple and waited for the pleasant fog to envelop her. And anyway, it would help clear the hangover that had bugged her all day, the nagging pain in the temple that had refused to go away.

She slumped into her only armchair and put the TV on, assaulted by Day-Glo, glitzy entertainment. Saturday evening fodder. She flipped through channels till she found a history show. It didn't matter what it was. Anything but today.

The cosy past.

She laughed bitterly. Maybe Timothy was right.

This documentary was anything but cosy, though. It was about the history of the Sioux Indians. Though the narrator pointed out that they weren't called the Sioux anymore; they were called by their true name now, the Lakota. The Sioux was the name given to them by their enemies and it meant 'snakes'.

It was like a newsreader calling the French *the Frogs* or the Germans *the Krauts,* Kath thought.

It was so tragic, so sad. It mapped out in doleful terms their fight for survival against the encroaching white man.

The pain, the cold, the hunger.

And the slaughter. So much slaughter.

The lies and the broken promises, until they'd lost everything.

She had a book somewhere about this. A tiny, slim Penguin edition. She had bought it as a child with her pocket money. It was in a box somewhere with all the other books that she hadn't unpacked yet.

Her eyes fell on the bookshelf and the bottle of gin stacked there. It would be foolish and irresponsible to drink gin on top of the Xanax. She laughed at a joke forming in her head. Something about the spirit world and the Medicine Men in the documentary, and the gin and Xanax in her flat.

She made another cup of tea and took her coat off.

But wasn't there a kind of cosiness to this documentary? It framed the history as a tragedy, it made you feel sad, but it didn't make you feel angry. It didn't make you want to rage and fight against this injustice. There was a pleasant buzz to the tragic sadness you felt.

It was indulgent, like some cheap soap opera.

Liz would be in town right now getting drunk at the German market with her friends, Sian and Zara. That was what you were supposed to do on a Saturday night. Except Kath couldn't afford it.

She knew too many young women who were drunks. Maybe you sought out your own reflections. Maybe you were drawn to them because they were just like you, even though a part of them disgusted you.

But it was the end of a working week. Everyone needed a release. Everyone needed to blow off steam. A little drink made the world feel okay again. It tipped the work-life balance back in your favour. After a hard week at work, you deserved it.

Before the history of the Lakota people had reached its painful conclusion, she had poured herself a gin to fall into the spirit world.

— 10 —

The Greys were there first thing on Monday morning, practically hammering the door down. They piled inside and took up the desks to settle down for the day. This research, this looking into the past, was their post-retirement 9-to-5.

The weekend had gone by in a blur. Of course it had. When you worked Saturday, there was hardly anything left to call a weekend. She had spent Sunday morning in bed, hiding from the world, in the pleasant fug of doing nothing. But once out of bed, she'd been gripped by the desire to make a change. She'd unpacked all of her books and put them on the shelves, and it felt a bit more like she lived in the place.

When she wasn't manning the reception desk and dealing with research queries, she tried to find time to delve into her own research for the next exhibition. There were some records on Moseley Hall in the archives, and she put together a timeline: built by John Taylor, one of Birmingham's first industrialists; set on fire in the Priestley Riots of 1791; bought by Richard Cadbury in 1889, who presented it to the city as a children's convalescent home. The hospital became a geriatric unit in 1970 and was now an NHS community hospital offering general medical, sub-acute care and specialist stroke and brain injury rehabilitation services for inpatients and outpatients.

She drifted off.

The problem was it was boring.

She pulled out her notes on the murder.

In 1889, a local man, Matthew Hopkins, was convinced a local woman, Florence Cawley, was a witch. He had accused her of sabotaging his business and police had investigated. Nothing was proven. Hopkins filed a further two complaints against her, alleging vandalism and then witchcraft, at which point a local magistrate, outraged at laughter from the public gallery, had ordered Hopkins to desist and keep the peace.

When Florence Cawley had not been convicted, Hopkins set out one night to murder her. He set fire to her house in Moseley and she died inside.

The news report did not give Florence Cawley's address. Kath rushed over to the shelf loaded with fat, red *Kelly's Directory* volumes, one for every year of almost the last hundred. She took out the 1889 edition and leafed through to find the name.

Miss F. Cawley. 26, Leighton Road, Moseley.

A stone's throw from the dovecote.

Kath gripped her throat and thought she could almost smell the sharp waft of wood smoke.

The newspaper reported that Mr Hopkins had told the judge he was convinced Florence Cawley was the witch seen haunting the dovecote, which bordered the Alcester Road. He had seen her himself one night as he was passing, walking home from the Fighting Cocks tavern. He had positively identified the apparition as

Miss Florence Cawley, though the police had refused to listen. Mr Hopkins asserted that the investigating officer, a Detective Inspector Wm. Beadle, was involved in the conspiracy and was a party to dark forces himself. The judge had had to adjourn the court due to so much laughter from the public gallery.

Mr Hopkins was sentenced to death.

Kath looked up his death record in the microfiche collection and was surprised to find no record for him in 1889. Florence Cawley was there, but not her killer. Surely he would have been hanged at Winson Green prison that year? She scoured through the next few years and found nothing, almost about to give up, when his name appeared in the list of deaths for 1897. Not in Winson Green Prison but close by at Winson Green Insane Asylum.

Somehow, he had avoided the noose and been committed.

She ran a digital search on the Matthew Hopkins murder case in the archives. Though most of the archive was analogue, the referencing had been digitized. It led her to an entry she didn't recognize.

"Liz," she asked. "What are records that start with WMPA-SL? They're not on our list."

"Oh, we don't have them here. Not for another two years. West Midlands Police archives. They're at Steelhouse Lane. You can book an appointment, if you can be bothered. I usually get them to do it. Fill out a request form."

The thought was tantalizing. If she wanted to see the arrest reports on Matthew Hopkins, she would have to request to see them. Could she get some time off to pop over and root through their archives?

She looked up the number, picked up the phone and punched it in. It rang twice. She put the receiver down. She didn't have time for this. She needed to concentrate on this exhibition, not be led astray.

Timothy came and leaned over her shoulder. "Moseley Hall. Very good. Hope you're finding lots that's interesting."

"Yes. Lots."

He picked up the photocopied sheet of Victorian news type. '*Witch' Murder Trial Opens.*

"What's this?"

"Some local man saw what he thought was a witch at Moseley Hall and decided to kill her."

"That's a bit gruesome."

"Yes, but fascinating," she said. "Imagine, a man in Victorian England thinking a local woman was a witch."

"I'm not sure that's what we should be featuring," Timothy said. "It's rather grim."

"Don't people like a good murder mystery?"

"Simpler times, that's what our audience want. They want to be taken back to a better time. They want to be given a glimpse of the past before it all went wrong. They just want a bit of escape from all this." He waved his arm at the concrete expanse all around them.

"But the past isn't a simpler time. It wasn't all better then. It was dark and squalid and hard."

The Lakota, she thought. Could she put on an exhibition about the Lakota? There was a Birmingham connection after all.

"You talk like you've been there."

"I'm sorry?" What had they been talking about?

"The past," he said. "You talk like you've been there."

"Oh, no. Though, haven't we all been in the past? It's

where we spend all our lives."

She giggled at the thought.

It was true. She remembered hearing about other cultures who viewed time as something that happened behind you. In our culture, we pictured ourselves facing forwards, walking into the future, but these people viewed themselves walking backwards, looking at the past. It was more logical, because you couldn't see the future that hadn't happened yet, you could only see the past that had happened.

"Just keep it nice and simple," said Timothy. "By the way, any luck finding that film?"

"No. It's misfiled. It's not where it should be."

"That's a real shame," he said. "It's crucial to your exhibition."

He smirked as he walked off, humming a simple tune.

He'd hidden it. She knew it now. He'd misfiled it so she'd never find it. So she'd fail and he could appoint his friend to her job.

She picked up the phone and punched in the Steelhouse Lane number. In a few moments, she was through to their archivist.

"Hello," she said. "My name's Kath Bright. I'm at Birmingham Central Library in the Local Studies department. I'd like to book an appointment to view something in your archive, please."

— 11 —

The archivist at Steelhouse Lane police station arranged an appointment for a week on Tuesday, frustratingly far away. In the meantime, Kath set up a trip to Moseley Hall. She cleared it with Timothy, though he hummed and hawed about her technically having an afternoon off.

"I have to go there some time," she said. "And it's work."

In the end, he let her leave at two on a Wednesday, when it was always quiet, and she caught her usual bus home but remembered to get off at the stop right opposite the dovecote.

The brooding presence disturbed her again. She frowned and put her head down and crossed the busy street, swerving into the driveway that led down to the hospital building, hidden behind trees.

She came through to a great expanse of lawn and a path leading down the hill. She passed a couple of pre-fab bungalows, which seemed to be administrative outbuildings, and on down to Moseley Hall, an 18th Century mansion now crowded by new glass-fronted annexes either side.

She talked for an hour with a hospital press officer who dug out some fact sheets regarding the history of the place. Nothing Kath hadn't already seen. They paused in the hallway. There were paintings that were of interest. She asked about making copies. If only she could borrow the actual paintings. That would be something.

Then the press officer walked her up the drive from the grand, expansive stately hall at the foot of the hill, up to the pre-fab huts. Half way up and to the right, and then winding left to the top of the hill where the dovecote loomed.

There was something about this journey, the pattern of it, winding their way up a hill, through various stages to the crest. Something that felt familiar. Something that felt like a dream.

The press officer pushed through a gate to a half-acre of gardens that were fenced off, and introduced her to a pleasant old lady from the Moseley History Society.

She showed Kath around the box-hedged gardens and explained that she and some other volunteers maintained the dovecote and the cowshed, tending to the gardens all year round. "It's sort of a second home."

Kath found it difficult to concentrate on what she was saying. It was as if someone was playing loud music nearby. No matter how interested you were in what they were saying, you couldn't cut out the music.

After a little while, the lady waved Kath away.

"Have a look round," she said. "Explore."

Kath wandered off and was drawn to the tower. That hum of energy again, as if it was radiating… something. She wasn't sure what.

She circled it, taking in its dimensions. A beautiful

Victorian red brick tower, octagonal. There were arches that looked like they might once have been windows, though it wasn't clear if they were just decorative. A wooden staircase up the side led to an exhibition room.

Kath reached out to touch the red brick surface and choked, gasping for breath.

The stone sucked the air from her lungs.

A punch to the guts.

Someone turned the lights out.

She blinked and stumbled, struggling to see. A white blizzard. Peering into the swirl of snow, she made out the surroundings. The dovecote next to her, the cowshed over there, the fence and the road beyond it. All covered in a sheet of blue snow. The air alive and teeming.

It was snowing. It was snowing at night.

The fence had changed. It was wrought-iron, chest high, with spikes. Hadn't it been a wooden fence of thick, square-cut timber before?

She gagged on the smell of pig manure. Rank and fetid. Pigs snuffled in the lower part of the dovecote.

She backed away, stumbling backwards, clumsy feet crumping through long grass heavy with snow, wanting to escape the tower, but also longing to hold onto it, as if it was both the sea that would drown her and the lifebelt that would save her.

A voice cried out behind her, a man's voice yelling involuntary fear.

She turned and saw her frosted breath in a cloud around her face.

A black-bearded man stood beyond the wrought-iron railings, wearing a derby hat, suit and waistcoat, a thick scarf around his neck. A grey apparition in the swirling storm. He shouted out in fear again — no words, just a primal yell — and raised his arm to point at her.

She didn't know what to do. She was about to call out to him, to tell him it was all right. But it wasn't all right. Nothing about this was right.

When she opened her mouth, no words came. She choked on air, and stumbled, falling backwards, her feet tripping in the snow, slipping, trying not to fall. She reached behind to break her fall, her fingers feeling the cold stone.

A blinding light. She blinked. Bright day, green grass, no snow. The man was gone. Beyond the wooden fence, a stream of rush hour traffic.

"Did you see the exhibition inside?"

The nice old lady from the Moseley History Society. She pointed up at the tower. The wooden steps that led up to a door halfway up the tower and an exhibition room.

Kath nodded and gasped for breath. "Yes, really good."

The old lady stared.

Kath said, "I have to go now. Thank you."

She rushed away, pushing through the gate, and was marching up the hill in moments. As she came to her house, she put her hand to the front door and paused for breath.

On her sleeve, she noticed a snowflake, its intricate pattern, delicate, trembling. Real physical proof that she had been there. It was not snowing now in 2008. But it had been back then. With her free hand, she tried to reach into her coat pocket, awkward, fumbling, to take out her iPhone. She turned it on and trying to angle it, to get a photograph, to get proof. If all of this was a delusion, she could show people the photograph.

Look, here, is that a snowflake?

It faded, melting into her sleeve.

She fumbled to open the camera app, and tried to frame it, but just as she clicked to take the picture, it was gone.

— 12 —

She sat on the other side of the bus on the way to work the next morning, so that as it passed the dovecote she could cover her eyes and pretend it wasn't there.

Although that nagging voice in her head kept telling her she was crazy, delusional, and just one visit to the doctor away from being committed to Winson Green asylum, she knew now with absolute certainty that it was real.

It was real.

The photo of the snowflake hadn't come out, but her sleeve had been wet, and it could only have been from the snow. The snow that hadn't been falling at all. Not here and now. Not this month. Her suede boots too were lined with a salty tidemark which could only have come from walking through snow.

It had all just been too concrete to be an illusion. There had been too much detail. She had felt the cold, the snow around her feet, the air billowing with snowflakes. And the smell of the pigs in the base of the dovecote, the stench of it making her gag. She just didn't think she had the imagination to create an illusion so vivid.

In her lunch hour, she booked one of the computers on the first floor lending library and Googled *timeslips*. She read about the famous case of two English women in 1901 who had slipped into the past at Versailles. Wandering lost in the gardens, and both noticing the strange change in atmosphere — depressing and unpleasant — they encountered a gardener dressed in an old-fashioned smock and a tricorn hat. One of the women noticed a lady sitting in a meadow, drawing, and later identified her as Marie Antoinette from a portrait. The other hadn't seen this woman. The delusion had been vivid, they had both experienced it and written about it separately. So not a delusion at all, unless it was all an elaborate deception.

An off-duty policeman visiting Liverpool in 1996 had turned into Bold Street, looking for the HMV store, but entered a strange 'oasis of quietness.' The street was not what he expected. A small 1950s box van nearly ran him over, and the people around were dressed in clothes from fifty years ago, all except for one girl whose handbag had a popular brand name on. They both walked into an old-fashioned clothes store that instantly transformed into the modern bookstore he'd been looking for. The man asked the girl if she'd seen what he had seen and she replied, "Yes. I thought it was a clothes shop. I was going to look around, but it's a bookshop." They had simply turned a corner and walked into fifty years ago.

In May 1973, a Norwich teacher experienced a timeslip into what appeared to be the remote past of Clava Cairns in Scotland. It was not until she leaned back against one of the standing stones that the extraordinary transition into the past took place, 'as though a switch had been thrown.'

Kath read each story with wonder and marvelled at the details that so matched her own experience.

She found a newsgroup chat room in an obscure corner of the Internet discussing timeslips and alternate dimensions. So many people talking of near death experiences, their lives changed significantly from the moment they had absolutely thought they were going to die. One was so certain of death because he was standing in the road with a truck hurtling towards him, no escape, and then he was elsewhere, as if he had died in one dimension and slipped into an alternate dimension where he had not been killed by a truck and was somehow now living that alternate reality with the full memory of his previous life.

All of the accounts one could dismiss as the ramblings of the psychotic and delusional. But they seemed so sure of their experiences, and absolutely specific in the details. So many similar incidents, too curious and strange to invent.

Her hour was up and she hadn't had lunch. She rushed back up to the sixth floor to take her post, her belly rumbling.

An old lady came to the front desk and plonked herself down in the seat facing Kath. Fidgeting. Wrapped up warm in a camel hair coat, woollen scarf and hat. She took off her mittens and smiled. A warm smile. A nice old lady. The kind you would want as your grandma.

For a startled moment Kath tried to place her. A face she knew. Kind, grey eyes.

She had dreamed her face: an old lady in a Dickensian nightmare, an old lady on New Street calling her name, an old lady smiling across at her now.

— 13 —

"Hello, my dear," the old lady said. "I wonder if you can help me."

No. It couldn't be. She had never seen this woman in her life before. She couldn't have seen her in a dream.

Or perhaps. What if she'd seen her before somewhere, a face in the street, hardly registered, and that face had fallen into her dream?

"Hello?"

"Yes. I'm sorry," Kath stammered. "That's what I'm here for."

"I'm rather new to this part of the library," the old lady said. "I've never been up here. And I'm wondering how it all works."

There was no recognition in this old woman's face. She was just a random face in the street that had found her way into a stupid dream.

"Is there something specific you're looking for?"

It was usually a death. The death of a relative, a distant relative. They were usually trying to find out how they got here, trying to fill out the details of the line that had brought them to this point, fill in the blanks of that family history.

The old lady pulled out a slip of paper, unfolded it, and read from her notes. "This might seem rather strange, but I wonder if you can tell me how I find out about a famous visitor to Birmingham. In the past, I mean."

"That depends," Kath said, "on how famous."

Don't say Charles Dickens, she thought. *Please don't say Charles Dickens.*

"Oh, quite famous. It was Charles Dickens."

The chair shifted under her, like she was on a ship and the sea had flooded in, everything floating.

"Well, that, er, shouldn't be too, ah, difficult."

"I have a library card," the old lady said, putting the plastic credit card on the table.

Hudson, it said. *Mrs. L. Hudson.*

Mrs Hudson read from her notes. "He came to read *A Christmas Carol* at the Town Hall just over there. Christmas 1844. The first time he'd ever read it in public, apparently. Imagine, being there to hear that."

Kath smiled at the thought. Charles Dickens right here, reading his most famous story.

"But I'm certain he came before that, a year before he wrote *A Christmas Carol.* Christmas 1842, in fact."

Kath keyed in the search terms, her fingers a blur, not connected to her in any way. A page of results flowed down her screen.

"It's possible he came to give a speech," the old lady said. "Perhaps at the Birmingham and Midland Institute around the corner. I know he did that a few times."

"I only have a reference to a speech he made at the Birmingham and Midland Institute in 1869. That's not the date you're looking for."

"No. That's nearly thirty years too late."

"Are you sure he was here before 1844?"

"I'm absolutely certain of it."

So hot. No air. There was something about her certainty. As if she'd seen him herself. Maybe she'd had a timeslip too.

Kath sniggered at the thought of this nice old lady being a time traveller. "Oh, this bit does say that when he came to speak in 1869, it was an educational organisation he'd supported since its beginning, sixteen years earlier. I make that 1853."

"That's too late. I'm looking for ten years before that."

Kath keyed in *Birmingham and Midland Institute* and found an entry. "Here we are. Founded in 1854."

"Yes, far too late, I'm afraid."

How forlorn she was, as if it was personal to her that Charles Dickens should have been in this city the Christmas before 1844.

"That's all I can see on this screen. But there may be more detail in some of the biographies." Kath pulled up some research for her and printed it off. "Down on the third floor in the Literature department. Reference only. You can't take them out, I'm afraid."

"That's all right. I can sit and read them right here. It's a pleasant enough place."

Mrs Hudson got up, pocketing her notes and her library card. "Thank you, you've been very helpful."

Kath didn't think she had. As she watched her walk off to the escalator and float down out of sight, she wondered why she hadn't started in the Literature department at first. Why would you come to Local Studies?

— 14 —

By mid afternoon, it was time for a tea break. She had fifteen minutes. She'd forgotten to make her peanut butter sandwich in the morning. She'd have to buy lunch. Sick with hunger, she thought she might nip down to the German market and maybe get a hotdog or something. If she rushed and there were no queues, she could easily do it.

She went down in the escalator and walked out through Paradise Forum past the McDonald's. There were some food stalls on the other side which wouldn't be as busy as those in Victoria Square and all down New Street. But they would be too expensive. She was best nipping into the Spar and grabbing a cheap sandwich or a pastie. If she was lucky, there would be something reduced.

The echo of voices in the giant atrium. It had once been completely open, just a concrete space, but more recently they had glassed the entire thing off and put in shops and bars, turning it into a mini-mall. A Wetherspoons pub took up one corner. It had once been a bloody awful Hooters bar. The smell of fish and chips made her swoon. It would take more than fifteen minutes to order and eat. There was no time. Jazz sailed through from the Yardbird pub just outside on the concrete plaza that led to Centenary Square and Broad Street.

The music cut out, and with it everything else. The chatter from the bars, the shoppers. The hubbub of voices. Just the howl of a fierce wind. It knocked her back and she tottered, waving to keep her balance.

It had all gone. No glass frames either side, just a great cavernous space, a chasm, the wind howling through it.

Where had the shops and bars gone?

A man, walking towards her, hunched over. A baggy suit. Shabby. Flared trousers, wide lapels, like something from the 1970s. Sideburns and long hair.

He glanced up at her, not expecting someone there. Surprised at her stillness, that there was a woman standing in the middle of this concrete cathedral. He looked twice, frowning. Like she was a weirdo. He walked on, quickening his step, platform shoes clumping on concrete.

A great void.

And then the noise rushed in. The Spar store was there in the corner. The Nando's behind. A mobile phone cover stall in the middle of the atrium. The Wetherspoons bar in the corner and the pungent waft of fish and chips. The trail of people filing through.

It had all gone, just for a moment, and now it was back.

As though a switch had been thrown.

She clutched her belly, almost doubled over, and staggered back to the library.

She wasn't hungry anymore.

— 15 —

For the rest of the afternoon, Kath tried to busy herself with work. Then she caught herself. Her hand shaking, her heart beating in her throat, that tremulous feeling of panic.

The present had been ripped away. Everything down there in Paradise Forum, all the bars and shops all the people, had all been ripped away as if some giant God had wiped it off the face of the earth, leaving just her in that cavernous empty space, leaving just her back then as it was in the 1970s.

It didn't make any sense.

The only sense it made was that she was mad.

She didn't think she could take it anymore. She had to get away. Get home and lie down and hope that this nightmare would be over when she woke up.

Local Studies was quiet. She left her desk and walked up the spiral stairs to the research room. Liz was fetching something from the back room. Kath turned and looked around the room, just hoping that all these people would call it a day and file out so she could ask Liz to go downstairs and cover for her.

A handful of Greys quietly working at the various

desks. And one younger man, alone at a table, a box file open and the contents splayed out before him. Old-fashioned looking, a bow tie, his moustache waxed to points.

With a shiver of recognition, she realized he was the man she had seen in the phantom room.

He was sitting right there. A ghost among the Greys.

Was it him?

The same moustache. A similar look.

She tiptoed over to his desk. He sensed her approach and looked up, surprised.

Think of an excuse. "Er… the Moseley Hall papers," she said. "Was that you?"

Her voice low. Just in case he wasn't really here and only she could see him, so people didn't see her talking to an empty chair.

"I'm sorry?" he said.

He didn't sound like a ghost. He sounded perfectly normal. But then what did a ghost sound like?

She glanced around the room. No one seemed to think it strange she was talking to this man or to an empty chair. "Oh. I thought it was you. I'm sorry, I must have got it wrong."

The man took out a handkerchief and wiped his nose. "Excuse me," he said. "I have a very bad cold."

He was just a man. Not a ghost. Just a man wiping his nose with a silk handkerchief, fighting off a cold. He was dressed a little old-fashioned. A lot old-fashioned. He was one of those young fogeys, just like her boss, Timothy. These young men trying to dress like their grandfathers.

His library card on the table. She craned her neck to read.

Mr R. Mitchell.

"I'm sorry, Mr. Mitchell. I thought you were someone else."

"It's Mitch," he said, wiping his nose. "Just Mitch."

She wasn't sure why he'd said that. She walked away, back to the desk. Still no Liz, so she went through to the back room and found her up a stepladder, filing a cardboard box on a high shelf.

"What is it?" Liz said. "You look like you've seen a ghost."

Kath allowed herself to smile. "No not a ghost. But I'm feeling rather ill."

"You look awful. Sorry."

"Yes. I thought I'd go home."

Liz checked her watch. "Yes, do it. There's not long to go, anyway."

They filed out back to the research room. Relief flooded her, and she realized just how much she needed to escape.

"I'll leave this lot up here."

They headed for the spiral staircase and Kath glanced over at Mitch.

He was gone.

The table was empty. No papers strewn about, no box file, no Mitch. He had disappeared.

"Where's he gone? Mitch, the guy who was sat there researching?"

She had been in the back room for 60 seconds, no more. There was no way he could have cleared up and left in that time. And there was no indication that he had returned the box file of research papers.

"Which guy?"

"You know, the old-fashioned guy with the waxed

59

moustache? Pointy tips. Like Salvador Dali."

"No. I don't know who you mean."

"He was in here, just a minute ago."

That blank look, trying to agree with her, searching her mind for a memory that might make it seem that Kath wasn't crazy. But there was nothing. "No, I don't know who you mean."

She was crazy.

Either that or she had talked to a ghost.

— 16 —

She got up on the Saturday morning feeling lighter, as if none of it had mattered. As if she could handle this whole seeing ghosts thing. Maybe she had just needed a good long sleep.

She had got home early on Friday and fallen straight into bed, waking with that luxurious feeling of having had exactly the right amount of sleep. A rare feeling.

It was the Moseley Farmers' Market, the last Saturday before Christmas. She decided to go along, enjoy herself and forget about everything, about the dovecote and about Darren and about ghosts.

It was a short walking to Moseley Village, but she took the long way around, first walking in the opposite direction towards Kings Heath and turning up Valentine Road, till she came to the great terracotta Gothic church at the island and turned up School Road. She crested the hill and walked down to turn into Oxford Road. The pleasant back streets of Moseley. Another church ahead. She thought it was St. Mary's at Moseley, but no that didn't have a spire. St. Mary's had battlements. And this was a tall Gothic church on Oxford Road. St. Agnes. As she passed it, St. Mary's came into view.

She turned and found herself on St. Mary's Row just above the crossroads of Moseley village. She walked down and saw the stalls all over the village green and the slip road and right up the pavement towards the Fighting Cocks pub. A cluster of market stalls and a crowd of people browsing between them. Christmas music playing from a loudspeaker.

She wasn't one to get slushy and sentimental about a bit of tinsel and the sound of sleigh bells — she suspected she might be a cynic at heart — but the Farmers' Market was nice. It was busy and there were some interesting stalls. You could get an ostrich burger and hot chocolate with marshmallows, and there was an amazing stall selling French cheeses with a half-hour queue.

There was a line of stalls on the other pavement on the opposite side of the road. She crossed over and found that they were all arts and craft stalls. She was drawn to a vintage clothes stall and looked for some 1960s dresses, stroking the fabrics on the rail.

A familiar voice. An old lady running the stall chatting to a customer.

Kath glanced across. It took a moment to place her. Yes, the old lady in the library who'd come in to ask about Dickens.

The old lady from her nightmare.

She was wrapped up warm in a great big overcoat and a woolly hat, drinking hot chocolate from a Styrofoam cup, chatting warmly. And then Kath pieced it together. The stall was right outside what she thought was a fancy dress shop. Hudson's Vintage Clothing. Mrs Hudson. This was her shop.

That was where she'd seen her before. This vintage

clothes shop. She's been here, before she'd moved to Moseley, looking for old 1960s dresses. She's been to this shop and seen this woman. And this woman had found her way into Kath's dream. It all made sense.

Kath walked on, right up the row of stalls, and crossed at the zebra crossing to the French café. She walked on up away from the market, drawn to the Prince of Wales pub. Too early for a drink, so she went into the antiques store, Buygones, next to it.

The bell above the door chimed.

She stepped inside and the bell above the door chimed. A pleasant jumble of junk. She wandered around, wondering if she might find something to furnish her new flat amongst the pleasant jumble of junk. After Christmas, when she had some money. It was all a bit too expensive, but she circled the store and headed towards a man reading a book behind the counter.

The ghost from the library.

Moustache with waxed tips.

He looked up from his book. Hesitant recognition between them.

"Hello," he said uncertainly.

"Hello," she grinned.

He cocked his head to the side, trying to remember.

"Research room, up the spiral staircase."

He snapped his fingers. "Oh, the library."

"Yes, that's me. Library girl."

"It's always strange when you see someone out of context."

"Yes, like they're a ghost or something."

He frowned, not quite understanding. "Er, yes I suppose."

She shrugged and smiled. It all made sense now. The ghost in the library who dressed like a Victorian. He wasn't a ghost at all. He was an antiquarian.

"See you again then," she said.

She bounced out to the chime of a bell, back down through the street market, all Christmassy and giddy.

He wasn't a ghost, just an antiquarian.

— 17 —

Her appointment at the police archives came on Tuesday morning, and she was lucky that Timothy was away for a meeting. She ran it by Liz, who said it was quiet so she could slip away for an hour. So she found herself walking across town and calling in on Steelhouse Lane Police station.

The grand Victorian building, which had once been the main police headquarters in the city, had been replaced by the tower block of Lloyd House sometime in the 1970s.

Once it would have been imposing but it was now crowded out by bigger buildings on every side.

She stepped inside to a normal police station reception, people waiting to report crimes, dossers being processed, the moans and complaints echoing down the corridors. If you came here, something in the dark shadows of the city had touched you, or you were part of the city's dark edges. It had always been this way.

A police officer came for her, introducing himself as Sergeant Varley, a pleasant, rotund chap who'd been behind a desk for far too long. He had the look of someone pleasantly surprised. Perhaps they didn't have many young women come here. Maybe he liked redheads.

He took her along a landing lined with old cells. The place was crowded with a rowdy school party.

"It's one of our open days," Sergeant Varley said. "People like to come and see a Victorian lock-up."

They skirted round the kids and parents, their laughter echoing off blue walls, and Kath shuddered at the posters of old mug shots in each cell.

They went down a flight of iron stairs to the lower level and came out to a long, murky corridor with dingy yellow light, leaving the clamour of the open day behind.

It was chillier down here, the chill of the past. She felt just a little closer to the building's Victorian ancestry.

He led her to an old cellar door and rattled his bunch of keys. They stepped into a vast room lined with metal shelves piled high with box files. The entire centre of the room looked like someone had tried to recreate the Manhattan skyline with a collection of reclaimed filing cabinets.

"It's a bit cold in here," he said. "I'll get the heating on, but between you and me, it takes a while."

"I'll keep my coat on," she said.

He looked around the room, as if uncertain what to do about it all. "You can help yourself. I'll leave you to it."

"Are you sure?"

He sighed. "Well, in two years' time, all this will be yours. So you might as well get started on it."

He pointed to a desk. A green banker's lamp, just like the one she had seen in the ghost room up in the library. She was seeing them everywhere. They seemed to be in every film on TV, as if it was some private joke by set designers.

"The index is here," he said, patting a thick lever-arch file on the desk. "But it's all pretty obvious and makes sense. There's a photocopier over there."

In the corner, a photocopier that looked even older than the ones in the library.

"Don't go mad with it," he said. "But copy what you need."

"Thank you," she said, sitting down and opening the file to get an idea of the shape of it all.

Sergeant Varley stood staring at the room, as if seeing it all for the last time. Then he gave a tight smile, nodded and walked out.

Kath searched through the index, trying to find police records, anything on the murder. There was a detailed list of arrest records and an archive of mug shots. The idea of seeing a photograph of the murdered woman or even the killer, made her heart beat faster.

She found a reference to Matthew Hopkins and dug through a filing cabinet to find the case file stuffed with interrogation reports and statements.

She pulled out yellow paper, crisp and brown at the edges as if it had been baked in an oven. Each sheet was full of close written script, so neat it looked like print, the type of cursive font you could choose on a computer if you wanted to design a fancy invitation. How could people write so decoratively and with such care? She imagined some Victorian police sergeant writing this out, dipping his fountain pen in an inkwell, perhaps in one of the rooms upstairs.

For a while, it was just about deciphering the text, and not appreciating the full meaning, but she settled into the rhythm of the story. What emerged was a tale of dark superstition and locals thinking this woman, Florence Cawley, was a witch and needed to be burnt.

Kath shook her head and whistled. In that day and age. There hadn't been a witch trial in Britain for a hundred years, but still the dark superstition persisted. It was supposed to be an age of enlightenment — Victorian progress and industry — and here you had a little pocket of the Middle Ages in a modern city.

Well, a village on the edge of a modern city.

Matthew Hopkins' statement was full of bluster and self-justification. He had complained about Florence Cawley's persecution of him several times and the police had ignored him.

I insist that the deceased, Miss Florence Cawley, is a red-haired witch who has sabotaged my livelihood with her spells and incantations.

Kath stroked her fingers through her red hair. What was it with redheads? Why did the world unload their fears onto them?

My bakery has failed entirely due to Miss Cawley's witchcraft. I regard the evidence as irrefutable and wish it to be put on record that the police have ignored me on this matter. I warned them, as a dutiful citizen, so it entirely their fault that this has happened. I have taken the law into my own hands, when really it is the responsibility of the police to protect the community from this witch. I believe I have saved Moseley from her dark arts, and should be rewarded with a medal, not persecuted with prison.

His exalted sense of his own importance shone through in every line of the rambling statement, as interpreted by the recording officer. She wondered if the police officer taking down Hopkins' statement —

Detective Inspector Wm. Beadle, she noted — had deliberately written it out, so it was obvious that Hopkins was insane. Or if he had believed in Hopkins.

This was the thing, she thought. How many men at that time were willing to believe that a woman could be a witch? Hopkins believed it, so why not the police? Just how safe was any woman at that time from the accusing finger of a man? Just how much sympathy would any woman get from a Victorian policeman?

None of that mattered, in the end, because Florence Cawley wasn't asked to defend herself or make a statement. Florence Cawley was dead.

Photographs of arrest subjects were kept apart from the statements. All the photos were kept together in a separate file, so Kath had to find the reference number that matched the statement and then go through the extensive archive.

She came to a batch for that particular month and pulled them out, her heart beating.

She would see his face.

A large cardboard box crammed with photographs, each one separated by tracing paper. She heaved the box onto the desk and rifled through them. Scores of Victorian mug shots, men and women, old and young, sometimes children, all with the dazed look of bomb survivors, the quizzical expression that said *why me? How has this happened? How did I fall into this?* As if none of them quite believed in their own guilt. As if none believed they had actually committed any crime.

She stopped at Matthew Hopkins' arrest photograph.

A man in a derby hat, black beard, suit and waistcoat. Eyes defiant. Proud bearing, as if posing for a family portrait as the proud patriarch, not a murderer in a police station.

She knew his eyes, the curl of his lip. He had been wearing a thick scarf around his neck when he had shouted out in fear. A primal yell. A grey apparition in the swirling storm.

Her vision at the dovecote. The man who had shouted at her from the street.

This was him.

This was the man who had murdered Florence Cawley.

Kath stared into his eyes for a good while, remembering how he had shouted at her. It couldn't have been a delusion. She couldn't have imagined that man in the snow, only to see him here on this photograph.

She took the photograph and the statements to the photocopier and copied it all. The photograph came out reasonably well.

Her eye was drawn to a reference number scribbled at the foot of the statement. Written in a different hand, not the fancy cursive handwriting of the officer who had taken the statement, but someone else. Much plainer handwriting, more modern. A string of numbers and letters.

A reference to another statement.

She searched for it through the filing cabinets and eventually found it in the arrest reports from the month before the murder. A statement by Florence Cawley, who had been arrested after an altercation with a local baker, Matthew Hopkins.

A short statement. Simply telling how she had had an argument in the street when Hopkins had confronted her. She had gone to his house to have it out at his door.

Neighbours had witnessed the shouting match. Hopkins said she had attacked him, but witnesses said it was nothing more than an argument.

There was another reference number at the bottom of the statement. A reference to an arrest photograph.

She ran over to the shelf and dug it out. The box right next to the blank space where she'd pulled out the previous box of photos. She took it to the table and rifled through it.

And there it was.

A photo of Florence Cawley.

A young woman, defiant glare, chin jutted forth, proud. Holding up a blackboard with her name and age chalked on it.

Kath stumbled up.

Her chair fell behind her.

The woman in the photograph was her.

The woman in the photograph was Kath Bright.

— 18 —

She had the presence of mind to photocopy the statement from Florence Cawley and the photograph.

The photograph of herself.

She crammed the photocopies into her bag, threw all the original documents back into the boxes and folders, and shoved them back into the filing cabinets and onto the shelves. She rushed out, slammed the door, and ran down the long corridor, up the stairs, rushing breathless through the police station reception area.

Sergeant Varley called after her. "Hey! Did you find what you wanted?"

She turned, caught. "Yes. Yes. Thank you very much. I just realized I have a meeting I forgot about."

"Righto," he said, waving.

She ran out to a blast of crisp winter air that scorched her lungs. As if she hadn't breathed since she had seen herself.

She rushed back to Chamberlain Square and the Central Library, dodging the lunchtime pedestrian traffic through the financial district, her mind racing.

These were not hauntings at all. They were not ghosts from the past. They were timeslips. It wasn't the past intruding on the present. It was her slipping back into history.

She was Florence Cawley.

Somehow. In some impossible way. Impossible, yet she had the evidence in her bag. A photograph of herself from a hundred years ago.

But if she was Florence Cawley, it meant she had been murdered in the past. Matthew Hopkins had murdered her in her house, set fire to her, burned her alive. Somehow, she, Katherine Bright, would go into the past and live there as Florence Cawley. And Matthew Hopkins would murder her. Somewhere in her future. A hundred years ago.

She clutched her throat as she rushed into the Central Library building and stabbed at elevator buttons to take her up to the sixth floor.

How was it possible?

The elevator doors slid open and she rushed out to take her place at the reception desk.

Timothy was there.

"Oh, hello Katherine. Nice of you to join us."

"I was just…"

He crooked his finger and nodded towards the back room. She followed him through and closed the door.

"I can't have this," he said.

"It's fine, I was just —"

"Spare me the pathetic excuses," he said, holding up his palm. "You've been skiving off to do some ridiculous research at Steelhouse Lane police station. Something I specifically told you not to do."

She stared at her shoes. He had probably got it out of Liz.

"It's not a very good start to your new job, and I

should remind you that you are on a probationary period. I should also remind you there are only three days left before we break for Christmas. I absolutely expect you to have the materials together for your exhibition before we break up. I want to see a detailed plan before the office party on Friday afternoon. Do I make myself clear?"

She looked up at his stupid red face.

He was smirking. Like he knew she would never do it.

There was no time to pull it all together, not in three days. She was doomed, as good as sacked.

And he knew it. It was as if he rather liked the idea of sacking someone for Christmas.

"Yes," she said. "Perfectly clear."

"Get back to work," he said. "And if you have to get the exhibition together outside of your desk duties, then you'll just have to work through the night."

She checked his face again, for any kind of hint that he might be thinking he could also stay the night with her. But there was nothing. Nothing but a pompous young man who wanted to be some sort of Victorian factory owner.

She slunk back to the reception desk and took her post. The usual afternoon crowd of Greys. There weren't many enquiries for the afternoon — as if they sensed that she needed the space — so she worked on the exhibition. A stack of boring images to be pulled from the archives and each one catalogued so they could be replaced. The boring, humdrum history of a country manor that had become a hospital.

She thought of how she might smuggle her murder story into the exhibition. Perhaps the mug shot of herself.

The face of a murdered woman from 100 years ago.

Her own face.

She could make it like some weird art installation; the self-portrait of a murdered woman at the centre of it all: the curator's own face.

Portrait of the Artist as a Victorian Murder Victim.

What would they say about that?

Timothy's stupid smug face spluttering outrage when he discovered it.

But that wouldn't happen. He would have his beady eye over every single detail of the exhibition before it was opened and he would take out anything remotely disturbing. The past was a cosy refuge from the present.

The man with the waxed tip moustache was there again, sitting at a table with reams of paper spread out around him. The antique shop owner. What was his name? Mitchell. Mr. R. Mitchell. *Mitch,* he'd said. He had the same moustache as the man she'd seen in the room upstairs. The room that wasn't there.

Was it him?

No. He was just a young fogey like Timothy.

An elderly lady came and sat with him and Kath let out a little moan as she recognized her. Mrs. Hudson. The Dickens lady who ran the vintage clothes shop.

So they knew each other. The old lady was researching Dickens and the young fogey researching God knows what. Perhaps he was helping her. He had an antique shop in Moseley and she had a vintage clothes store 100 yards away from his. It wasn't so strange that they would be here together.

She thought for a mad moment they might be sinister figures from the past coming to take her back to 1889.

Coming to take her back to where she could be burnt as a witch. She had seen them both in the past, after all.

Perhaps this was her mania. That she saw people and grafted their faces onto memories. Perhaps it was a recognized condition, some form of paranoid delusion. A doctor could tell her this. She was seeing quite innocent people and her scrambled mind was putting their faces into memories — memories that weren't real. Nightmares. Dreams she'd never had. Her mind was making them up on the spot and she only thought they had happened to her yesterday, last week.

This was how you ended up in Winson Green Insane Asylum.

But no, she laughed to herself. She wasn't going to end up in any asylum. That wasn't her fate at all. She was going to be burned alive in 1889.

— 19 —

It was clear that Timothy wouldn't give her a chance. There was no point in trying to make the deadline. She would be sacked on Friday because she did not have enough to show him. So screw it, she thought. She would simply pursue her investigation

The only thing she could do was amass data. Collect as much historical evidence as she could, and work from there. It was what she was trained to do. It was her only skill.

She had Florence Cawley's name and the date of her death. From there she could look her up. She had already found the official reference to her death in the microfiche catalogue, and from there she got her birth date. There was no record of a marriage. She was a spinster witch.

It was approaching her tea break, so she rushed over to the Register Office, through Paradise Forum, over the bridge, across Centenary Square, to the old building facing the Repertory theatre. She spent five pounds on each certificate, the birth certificate and the death certificate, and took them back to her desk.

There was a daughter's name on the death certificate.

A curious thing. If Kath somehow was to go into the past and live in Victorian Moseley, she would have a daughter. She would have a daughter and call her Margaret. She couldn't imagine choosing that name for her own daughter. So perhaps the father had chosen it. Some man she was to marry in the future. In the past. But there was no record of a marriage. And it didn't make sense that Kath, who didn't look much older on the photograph shortly before her death, could have a daughter called Margaret, aged 20 years.

She searched on Margaret Cawley and found her birth date, but she wasn't there in the microfiche of deaths. She must have changed her name. She would have been married. Kath found her marriage date. Valentine's Day, 1912. She had married Charles Barrow. From there she found Margaret Barrow in the death fiche. She had died in 1921, aged 53.

It was too late to go to the Register Office and get the death certificate. They would be closing, and Kath had to stay at her post.

Timothy left at five and gave her a nod. Smirking as he entered the elevator.

She pondered how to find more information on Margaret Barrow without the death certificate. It was something of a dead end until the Register Office opened in the morning.

Wills. The record of wills. She found them in a set of giant ledgers bound in red leather. Every will and testament recorded. She found the relevant year and rifled through the pages to find to whom Margaret Barrow had left her fortune.

Something naggingly familiar in the name. Margaret Barrow. As if she had heard the name before. A celebrity of some kind? Had she become famous? Perhaps an actress.

Margaret Barrow had left a modest fortune to her surviving children. So her husband had died before. That was lucky. Or there would've been no record of her will. It would all have simply passed to her husband. £448 to be divided between her daughter, Claire Barrow, and her son, Thomas.

She repeated the process with both of those names. This was how you built a family tree: the painstaking trawl through the archives collecting names, rushing back-and-forth between the Register Office and the library, collecting birth, marriage and death certificates, looking up the names in Kelly's directories to find the addresses, weaving a thread of connections through generations.

And again that peal of familiarity. Claire Barrow. A name that seemed so familiar. Where had she heard it?

She looked up the birthdates and then the marriages, avoiding the mistake of going to the deaths first. Thomas Barrow had married Agnes Bates in 1933. And Claire Barrow had married the following year.

1934.

Kath stared at the name of Claire Barrow's husband.

Wilfred. Wilfred Bright.

A chill ran through her. Someone tapped her shoulder. She flinched. Looked around. There was no one left in the library. She'd had the entire sixth floor to herself for the last two hours. Rain pattered on the windows. She would get soaked going home.

Wilfred Bright.

There it was. That aching sense of familiarity. Barrow. That distant part of the family. A great grandmother she had heard of through family talk, when old aunties got together at funerals. Kath had heard it all and never been much interested.

But now she saw it.

Florence Cawley was not her. She only looked like her.

Here it was, in black and white, in true historical fact. You couldn't argue with it or dress it up as mystical mumbo-jumbo.

Florence Cawley was Kath's ancestor.

— 20 —

That night, Kath fell into bed as soon as she got home. She woke to bright dawn sunlight glaring through the window and lay sighing, luxuriating in the warmth on her face. She had slept well for the first time in months.

She got ready for work, humming and singing along to chart hits on the radio, and as the bus inched past the dovecote on the way to work, she felt nothing. No vibration, no hum of electricity, no disturbing visions.

She wasn't slipping into the past, the whole thing was crazy. She was related to a woman who had been murdered a hundred years ago. And that was all there was to it.

Florence Cawley was her great-great-great grandmother.

Kath had just been a little run down, working too hard. The stress of the break up with Darren, and moving house, everything really. It had all been too much. Her imagination had run amok. Stress could do that, surely? But that was over now. There was a logical reason for it all. She knew she was sane.

She would go into work and put together whatever she could. It was Wednesday morning. She had two whole days before the deadline. And yes, there was about three or four days' work, but if she gave it a go, she might have enough and Timothy wouldn't sack her.

She walked up the street through the German market, unable to quell that optimistic Christmassy tingle in her breast. It was sentimental nonsense, she knew, a drug to make you spend more money than you had, and people were necking palmfuls of the drug, even as the banks collapsed and the Government poured billions into the bankers' pockets to bail them out. There was a major recession about to hit, but it felt like everyone was ignoring it.

She understood it, because on a lovely crisp winter's morning like this, with sugary sweet Christmas songs blaring out on the street, and tinsel and glittering fairy lights everywhere, you could pretend there wasn't a giant cataclysm coming, an asteroid about to hit.

The Local Studies crowd on the sixth floor was thinning now that Christmas was a week away. There were notably less Greys hogging the desks — presumably, they were out shopping for grandkids' presents — so Kath managed to get a few hours of research time up on the seventh floor while Liz covered downstairs.

She ran through the photographic archive. It was a huge collection. So many fascinating photographs of the city, some of them as old as 1837. As soon as photography had been invented, photographers had been documenting the streets of Birmingham.

There were less photographs of Moseley, and very few of Moseley Hall, but she gathered what she could. The larger collection beguiled her, though, and she found herself sifting through reams of photographs and records of old paintings and drawings of the city.

This should be an exhibition, she thought. A pictorial history of the city, using illustrations, paintings, drawings, photographs, maybe even film. One great exploration of the city in pictures. The city as it had been seen by artists through history.

Breathless with excitement, she felt a pang of hunger and nipped downstairs to let Liz go off for lunch, as long as she returned with a sandwich.

Liz came back after an hour with a tuna and mayo baguette, smiling and slurring her speech just a little. Another meeting at the German market with her friends, drinking *glühwein*.

Kath wondered what it would be like to have friends you could do that with. She had never gathered around herself a group of girlfriends. For the first time she wondered if it was some lack within herself. She'd never belonged to a tribe. She was a lone wolf.

Liz asked how the preparation for the exhibition was going, so Kath ran her through everything she'd gathered. It wasn't much. Liz gazed and let out a *hmmm* every so often, and she'd run through everything she had in five minutes.

Desperate to fill the space, she blabbed on about the archive of photographs upstairs and the possibility of a really major exhibition covering the entire city.

"Yes, but…" Liz slurred. "That's not this exhibition."

She had wasted the whole morning preparing the wrong exhibition. It was no good working on a brilliant idea for the future if she messed up the one she was supposed to be delivering in two days. There would be no future exhibition if she didn't deliver this one!

"There's something else I've found," Kath said.

She pulled out the photocopies from Steelhouse Lane and told her the story of Florence Cawley. Slapping each birth and death certificate down on the desk, splaying the documents out. "Here," she said. "See. There."

She unfolded the family tree she had drawn and traced her finger down the line that connected Florence Cawley to Katherine Bright.

"Bloody hell," Liz said.

"You see? Isn't it amazing?"

"It's fascinating. Fancy that. You're related to her."

Kath stopped her mouth blurting out, *And I've been seeing the past too. Actually flitting back to Florence Cawley's time!* She held back and covered her mouth with her hand and coughed.

"It's a lovely personal story," said Liz. "Not that it gives you anything for this exhibition, mind. Still, you've got another couple of days to pull some stuff together."

Liz left, grinning to herself. Drunk, not malicious.

Kath pulled the Florence Cawley documents into the folder and stuffed it in her bag, ashamed of it now, wishing she'd never shared it. She looked at the paltry collection of references for the Moseley Hall exhibition and knew she'd have to spend the night in the library.

— 21 —

For her afternoon tea break, she rushed out to the paper shop at the top of New Street and bought two reduced-to-clear sandwiches, a tube of Pringles and an apple. She would need supplies to see her through the night. Hot food would be nice, but too expensive, and she couldn't imagine how she'd order pizza and get it delivered to the library.

She had a travel toothbrush and a little tube of toothpaste in a desk drawer to freshen up after lunch, so she would be fine in the morning. But she wouldn't be able to change or shower. She had food, though, and could make coffee all night if she wanted with the staff kettle.

Timothy left at six, making no reference to the deadline he'd given her. Liz walked out minutes later giving a cheery goodbye. After fifteen minutes of the home-time clatter of staff leaving down escalators and in elevators, the library fell silent and she had the sixth floor to herself. It spooked her, the enormity of it. She retreated up the spiral staircase to the smaller research room on the seventh floor.

She held her nose and submitted herself to the bland

research Timothy had ordered, following a trail of information through the photographic archives, sifting through images and cataloguing a particular picture of the hospital. After two hours, she sat back with a sense of triumph.

But there were about twenty more of those to go. Even working through the night, there was just no time. It was slipping away from her.

Something she had spotted earlier in the photographic archive intrigued her. She'd seen it in the morning. She checked her watch. Twelve hours ago. No. Thirteen. She had been at work most of the day. The building was consuming her.

She pulled out a set of photographs of the same view changing over time. There was a sheet of notes which explained that the photographs had been taken by a research scientist who'd had the idea to document the building of the Central Library, this building in which she stood now, by taking a photograph each month from the same spot. What he had done, though, was capture the old buildings that had been here before. He had captured them being demolished. The photographer had wanted to turn it into a time-lapse film but had died before completing the project. And now his photo stills were filed away in the concrete monolith he'd captured being built. No one would see them.

She flipped through the photos. It was almost a film. It could be made into a film. A time-lapse of destruction. It documented an extraordinary act of urban vandalism. The buildings that ringed Chamberlain Square were beautiful Victorian neo-Gothic structures. Where this inverted ziggurat now stood had been the old Mason College and next to it the Liberal Club. The photographs were from the 60s. It seemed astonishing that one could walk around Birmingham in the 60s and see such beautiful Victorian architecture.

Even more astonishing that the city fathers could knock it all down and replace it with this Brutalist abstraction. As you sifted through the photographs, you felt horror for the city's capacity to disfigure itself.

She was humming along to the distant tune before she became conscious of it; a thin thread of music floating through the building.

Whistling. Someone was whistling.

It was gone 10 o'clock. Probably one of the security guards. She wondered if she'd be told off for staying so late. But her boss had pretty much told her she'd have to work all night. So it must be that some staff did work late.

She followed the sound. Through the door marked *Staff Only*, out through the cavernous dark space of the reference stacks. The sound was coming from that same aisle where she'd seen the ghost room.

She crept forward and peered round the shelf.

The door at the end was back again, a green glow emanating from inside.

She inched forward and stepped through.

That same room lit by the haunting glow of green banker's lamps. A Victorian reading room. She expected to see him sitting there at the desk again. Mitch. Or the man who'd looked like him. But no one was in the room.

The sound came from beyond.

She crossed the room to the open door on the far side and peeped through.

A long, dark room with wooden benches, racks of test

tubes and glass bottles, Bunsen burners. A laboratory. A shaft of dim blue light from the door at the far end. The whistling too, echoing from there.

She crept across the laboratory and stepped out into a great corridor, tip toeing on the marble floor. A wash of blue light further down where the passage opened out.

She padded forward, trying not to make a sound, but let out a gasp as she came to a balcony that looked over a great ornate atrium. A giant staircase swept down three flights. The whistling echoed from somewhere down there.

"Here! You!"

She jumped, turned.

A man at the far end of the corridor, holding an oil lantern, its beam finding her, lighting her.

"What the bloody blazes?"

She backed off. He was between her and the door back to her own time.

"Stop right there!"

She turned and ran. Down the marble stairs.

"Stop!" he cried, his voice echoing like a gunshot in the giant vault.

She pounded down the stairs, her boots clattering on the marble, turning and screeching like a car taking a sharp turn at the first landing.

A shout from somewhere on that floor. Another man running towards her.

"Intruder!" the first man shouted, high up.

His dull beam of light followed her as she sprinted down the staircase.

"Hilly ho!" another shouted.

She was a fox chased by hounds.

She rounded the last flight of stairs.

A third guard came running out to stop her.

She dodged past him and pounded down to the vast chequered floor.

More voices. Footsteps running to her from dark corridors. The men above gunning down the stairs for her.

She ran to the giant doors, some twenty feet high, and pulled at the brass handle. It creaked open, to her shock, and she pelted through to the cold night, expecting to run down the stone steps of the amphitheatre, but it wasn't there.

It was a gaslit square fringed by Victorian buildings. In the middle of the square, the fountain she recognized, the Chamberlain monument, to the left the art gallery, but without the bridge, only a great open chasm where Edmund Street ran. Before her the Doric columns of the Town Hall.

Behind her, where the Central Library should be, a neo-Gothic palace: the building she'd seen in the photographs. Mason College. It had been demolished fifty years ago.

"Stop! Thief"

The men with lanterns stormed out of the building.

Kath turned and ran across the gaslit square.

— 22 —

She darted through the gap where the corner of the
Council House met the corner of the Town Hall. Not a
path but a street.

A horse and carriage thundered past but she squirmed
away from it, ran alongside it, cut across behind it. A
squelch of softness beneath her. A pile of horse dung in
the gutter. She skipped through it and into Victoria
Square.

Shouts behind her.

She had the urge to run and keep on running.

But she stopped dead.

It was not the Victoria Square she expected to see.
There was no Floozie in the Jacuzzi, no steps leading up
to the fountain, no statue of Queen Victoria, no
Iron:Man. Instead, a giant church squatted in the middle
of the square, and between it and the Town Hall an
open square with lanes and two small islands with statues
of city elders looking down.

She recognized them. They had been moved to the
steps of the amphitheatre, back in her own time.

Footsteps thundered on flagstones behind her.

Before her a row of buildings where the post office

should be. A theatre and Corbett's Temperance Hotel. A shudder of recognition.

She ran towards it, not knowing why, not knowing where she was running to. There was no escape from this. There was nowhere to run to. She considered running down the eerily gaslit stretch of New Street, like she had in her dream. This was different to that. No snow,

She dodged by Corbett's Temperance Hotel along the row and down the dark hill of Pinfold Street. A huge glowing presence down there. A giant dome. No, it was New Street Station. The old station. She ran down towards it. Those footsteps close behind her.

"Stop! Thief!"

A man walking up the hill towards her, nothing but a silhouette. He held his arms out wide to greet her, to stop her. As she barrelled towards him, unable to stop herself or to veer around him, he stepped forward, his face lit by a gas lamp.

Fedora hat, waxed moustache, white collar and cravat tie.

Mitch. Or a man just like him. He was crying.

"I'm so sorry," he said.

Then he punched her in the face.

— 23 —

She jumped awake and sat bolt upright, dizzy, feral, shocked to find herself on the sofa in the staff room, her coat over her.

She'd slept. A nightmare.

She couldn't remember going to bed. She had worked all night. She had no memory of stopping work and settling down on the sofa. It was a blank.

Or Mitch had knocked her out and carried her back to this place.

She threw the coat off and ran through the seventh floor research room, through the *Staff Only* door to the reference stacks, cold and grey and dim. Along the rows of shelves.

The room wasn't there. There was no door, just an expanse of concrete wall. There was no room beyond it lit by green banker's lamps. No door that led to Mason College.

Her guts churned and she bent over, retching, but held it back. Don't be sick here at work, you'd have to explain how you threw up in the reference stacks because you stayed overnight.

Gasping for breath, eyes watering, she noticed her

boots ringed with a tidemark of mud. One was coated in a thick crust of red clay. She snatched it off and held it to her face. The ripe smell of horse manure.

It had happened. It was no dream.

This was it. Physical bloody proof. This was not a snowflake melting on a sleeve. This was horse manure from a Victorian street, 120 years old.

She put her boot back on and ran, half hopped, to the photographic archive, digging out old illustrations of Victoria Square. It was called Council House Square then. She pulled out drawings and old photographs. The old buildings that lined Chamberlain Square. There they were. Mason College and the Liberal Club towered over the square just as they had last night. Council House Square was dominated by Christ Church. The sad grey statues of Wright, Priestley and Watt looked down from their plinths. Shabby Corbett's Temperance Hotel stood overlooking it.

All there exactly as she'd seen it. How could she have known all that when she'd never seen these pictures before?

Or was she fooling herself? Maybe she *had* seen the photographs before. Maybe last night she had seen the photographs and then imagined her jaunt into that past — maybe it hadn't happened the other way round. Maybe time was jumbled up in her head.

If you were mad, you could rearrange time in your head. This morning was really last week. A moment ago was really last year. This year was really a century ago.

She was losing it. A ragged edge to her days. Like the stitching on her cardigan fraying, she was unravelling.

But no. One of her boots was caked in horse manure.

She ran back to the staff room. Noises from

downstairs. Cleaners doing the morning shift, sweeping through the library. She would have some time to nip down to the toilets and have a wash, tidy herself up, put on some make-up. Make herself look like she hadn't slept here all night. But she wouldn't clean her boots. The horse manure was staying. It was proof of her sanity.

She pulled out the folder from her handbag. The photo of Florence Cawley.

She had called her to the past. Her ancestor summoned her, as if she were calling out over decades, sending out a distress signal. It had pulled Kath to her. Florence Cawley had somehow called for help across five generations.

Kath was meant to save her. Somehow, she had this power to flit through time. And Florence had called her. Florence had called for help. Kath was meant to save her.

But then again, a lingering doubt. Had her flit through time caused Florence to be killed? If she hadn't been pulled through time by the dovecote, Matthew Hopkins wouldn't have seen her that night in the snow, and wouldn't have thought it was Florence Cawley appearing and disappearing like a ghost. Like a witch.

It was her own fault that her ancestor had been murdered.

Because Katherine had slipped into the past, Florence Cawley had been burned alive in her house.

She put the photograph away and smoothed down her skirt, facing the day with grim determination.

She had to go back again and stop it.

— 24 —

She worked all day and did what little she could on the exhibition, but knew now that it was hopeless. She had no time to prepare enough for the meeting with Timothy the next morning, and she was not going to stay another night working in the library. Tonight she was going home, and then going back to save Florence.

If Liz noticed Kath was wearing the same clothes as yesterday, she said nothing. She was already detaching herself: one foot in the library, one foot on Dartmoor.

Kath drifted through the day, experiencing random waves of hyper-excitement and sudden slumps of depression. This was what 24 hours without sleep did to you. She noticed the effect, rode the waves of adrenaline, and quietly trudged through the swamps of exhaustion, detached from it, noticing it as if it was happening to someone else and she was merely an independent observer, clipboard in hand, noting down the effects.

She rode it through to 5 o'clock and walked out.

Chamberlain Squire was bustling, commuters streaming through, the food and craft stalls doing business. She skirted the amphitheatre, halted outside the steps of the art gallery and looked back up at the library. It had looked nothing like this last night, just the fountain monument at the centre of it. Mason College and the Liberal Club towering over the square. All of it lower, she realized now. There was no amphitheatre. Just a gentle rise from the fountain to the door of Mason College.

She shivered, pulled her coat around her and pushed through the crowds of Victoria Square, walking under the giant *Iron:Man* sculpture and down New Street, not looking down Pinfold Street, where she'd seen the giant dome of the old New Street Station.

As she caught the 50 bus home, she tried to imagine the great sprawl of the city as it was back then, a place she might explore. She giggled at the thought of going back anytime she liked. But should she? How safe was it? She had felt the air of violence last night. Even New Street, lined with grand Victorian buildings, had the stench of a murky slum, seething with dull threat. It wasn't the kind of place you might explore alone. She giggled again at the idea of it being a choice. Could she even control it?

As the bus came to Moseley village and climbed the hill towards Kings Heath, she stared out at the floodlit dovecote and felt its power, like a nightclub's booming bass resonating in her bones. This, she thought. This was how she'd do it. The dovecote was all she needed.

Stumbling into her flat, a wave of exhaustion swamped her and she fell into the sofa.

Hunger woke her, growling in her belly. The kitchen clock said 10 p.m. She had slept for four hours. She ate a microwave pasta bake and thought of how this might take hours to cook back then, and if anyone in Birmingham even knew what pasta was. Surely those rich Victorian gentleman heading to Italy on the grand tour had encountered pasta. It seemed absurd that they hadn't or that there might not be an Italian community in the city. It was something she could find out.

Again that insane giggle, as if it wasn't coming from her, as if it was a ghost laughing at her.

She thought of how to dress and prepare for this. A maxi-skirt that came down to her ankles. A long overcoat. What kind of hat? She had nothing that was appropriate, so she took a Paisley shawl and put it over her head. Did she need a weapon? He was a short man but bullish, thick fists. He was intent on murdering Florence Cawley and Kath would have to stop him somehow. But how?

She took a chef's knife from the cutlery drawer and slipped it into her coat pocket, hoping she wouldn't have to stab him, hoping that her mere appearance might be enough to scare him to death.

She stepped out into the dark. Cars parked up on the wide pavement area before her house. A number 50 bus sailed past down the hill. She gripped the shawl at her neck and walked up the hill towards Moseley, and then down the gentle slope, crossing the tarmac road by the Hope Chapel on the corner of Reddings Road, wondering if that would be there where she was going.

She felt the dovecote before she saw it. Humming louder than ever, vibrating in her breastbone as she got closer. It emerged behind the trees at the corner of the slip road that ran down to the hospital. Eerie in the floodlights. There was hardly anyone around. No one at the bus shelter in front of the telephone exchange next door. Down below, Moseley crackled with life, music from the bars, a few shadows walking up the hill towards her. A bus about to ride up.

She climbed onto the wooden fence and eased through under the top bar, like getting onto a horse.

No time.

She strode across frosted lawn, reached out to touch cold stone and fell through a century.

— 25 —

A blast of ice. She jerked her hand back. Moonlight on snow lit the scene, not floodlights. The stench of pig manure. The sound of them snuffling and grunting. The cowshed to her side, but no garden, no box hedges down the slope. She ran to the wrought-iron fence, as high as her neck, and heaved herself over, the spikes sticking into her. She fell into the street with a yelp. All wet, she brushed snow off and pulled her shawl closer.

No pedestrian crossing with lights and a signal box. No bus shelter. No telephone exchange. No music booming from the bars down in the village. As she crossed, she felt the grit under her boots. No tarmac, just a dirt road. But the same row of cottages immediately opposite and the same three-storey townhouses lining both sides of the road.

Turning into Tudor Road, she ran along a row of Victorian terraced houses, her footsteps crumping on snow, eerily lit by gaslight.

The same streets, the same rows of terraced houses. Of course it was all the same except for the gas lamps. This was the thriving urban Moseley of the turn-of-the-century, not some village in the dark ages. The only medieval thing from that time was Matthew Hopkins' seething mind, desperate to burn a witch.

She rushed on up the street and turned into Leighton Road at the end. A man passed her on the corner, muttered with surprise and tipped his derby hat, passing on. She didn't look out of place, perhaps, or he hadn't taken her in, snowblind.

She came to the house and checked the number on the red door.

Twenty-six.

Florence Cawley's house.

Her great-great-great grandmother was inside right now.

Kath wondered if she should knock the door. How would Florence react to seeing her double call in the night? A doppelganger. A presentiment of death. Could she explain to her ancestor what was going to happen? If she couldn't convince her of the whole *I'm from 100 years in the future* thing, surely she could explain that this man who'd been harassing her was tonight going to burn her to death?

She stepped forward, pushed open the small gate and reached out to knock the door.

It was open.

The front door was ajar, edged with a black slit.

Heart thumping in her throat, Kath pushed the door open and stepped into the hallway, her way lit by a shaft of moonlight through the stained-glass panel above the front door. Stairs before her.

A scuffle from upstairs. A muffled cry. A woman's voice.

Matthew Hopkins was already up there. He had her. So he had broken in and murdered Florence before setting fire to the house.

She still had time, surely? Or why was she back here at all?

She delved into her coat pocket, her fingers finding the plastic handle of the chef's knife, and pulled it out. It glinted silver in the moonlight.

No time.

She lurched for the stairs.

— 26 —

Kath stepped through the open door at the top of the stairs. A room lit blue by moonlight. A humped shape on the bed. She thought it was a giant pile of clothes, but it shifted, and within its black pile a face turned to her.

A man's face. Bearded. Matthew Hopkins.

And under him on the bed, Florence, squirming under his weight. A silent struggle.

Kath leapt forward, sliding the knife out of her pocket as she crossed the room in three steps and plunged it into his back.

It squelched and nicked bone. She felt it through the shaft of the handle. She pulled it out and he yelped, blood squirting from his back.

She thought he would slump and die on top of Florence, like he would if it were a movie, but he sprang up, roaring, an angry bear slashing at her face.

Kath fell back. The room turned upside down. Her skull cracked on the wall. The knife skittered across bare floorboards.

Hopkins dived across the room and was on her. His weight crushed her and she fought for breath. His thick fingers on her neck.

Florence leapt from the bed and staggered out of the door, down the stairs, screaming into the night.

Matthew Hopkins glared down, squeezing the life out of Kath's throat. A thread of spit came from his snarling mouth, dangling in the air and landed on her lips. She tried to squirm away but his brute hands held her fast.

Her fingers scrambled for the knife, just out of reach.

Black ink filled the room. She was drowning. She felt herself fading.

This was death.

This was what it felt like to die.

She looked up into his eyes and the last thought, before she sank into the blackness, was that Florence Cawley would live, not die.

Hopkins seemed to sense it.

He screamed in rage and pressed harder on her throat.

— 27 —

Kath woke in a white room. She glanced around in panic, wondering if this was a hospital or if this was death. Dim light.

Laughter. An evil cackle. She turned to the man who sat in the middle of the empty room. His bulk hunched over, his beard covered in spittle. He wore a white smock and it was only when he twisted to see her that she noticed his arms tied behind his back. A straight jacket. She looked around at the white walls and floor and saw it was a padded cell.

"You're here with me now," he said. "There's no escape, witch."

What was this? Some sort of purgatory, or the last dream of her dying consciousness? Her knees buckled and she slumped to the hessian floor.

Matthew Hopkins laughed. "I've got you now, witch!"

"I'm not Florence Cawley, you thick bastard," she spat.

"I know who you are, Katherine Bright." He cackled again, slobbering.

Kath felt his laughter creep down her spine. "How do

you know that?"

"I know all about you. You think you got one over on old Matthew Hopkins but you don't even know what you did."

She circled him, keeping to the padded walls, scared to get within spitting distance.

"You don't exist, Katherine Bright. Not no more."

"What do you mean?"

"You saved Florence Cawley, and that wiped you out. You were never born."

He roared with laughter and Kath felt the cold truth of it. She was cast adrift in the universe. Alone.

"You think you're alone now," he said, "but that's nothing compared to this."

"What do you mean?"

"You have no friends. Even that Liz girl. Oh, Meckle's going to get her. You wait and see."

This wasn't real. She was hallucinating. Hopkins was strangling the life out of her and this was her final delirious breath.

She hammered the door. "Get me out of here!"

"Your miserable dregs of a family you crawl to at Christmas. You won't even have that."

She turned to him. How could he know all this? "You don't know anything about my family."

"Neither will you, now. It ripples through time. Because you saved that bitch, you're not born. You're here with me. Forever."

She hammered at the door, her fists slapping on padded hessian. She had to wake up. This was too real. There was no way out.

Hopkins bellowed his evil laugh and rose to his feet with a great grunting effort. Slobbering through gritted teeth, he staggered towards her.

Kath dug in her coat pocket and felt the cold blade of the chef's knife.

She pulled it out.

Hopkins lunged at her, arms tied behind his back. "You can't get out!"

Kath jabbed the knife at him.

He barrelled right into her and knocked the knife through her grip, the blade slicing her palm.

She yelped in pain.

He stumbled and fell, shrieking, "You're mine now!"

Kath's eyes met his as she held up her palm. Her blood spurted, vital, alive, and splattered across Matthew Hopkins' face.

He screamed as she fell.

— 28 —

Her throat burned. Coughing, retching, she pushed herself up from wet grass, the knife still in her hand, blood oozing from her palm.

She stabbed the knife into the soil, rolled to a squat, ripped her scarf from her neck and wrapped it around her hand, drawing a tourniquet tight with her teeth.

The dovecote loomed above her, lit by floodlight. A 50 bus roared past down the hill to the village. A pedestrian crossing winked at her beyond the wooden fence.

She was back in her present.

She had rescued Florence Cawley, and then she'd been in Winson Green asylum with Hopkins. Had that been real or some nightmare half-world of her imagination? She had saved Florence and then been cast into Hell with Matthew Hopkins.

It wiped you out, he'd said. *You were never born.*

She dug into her coat pocket, pulled out her iPhone. Scrolling through her numbers, she pressed the word *MUM.*

It chirped in her ear and she waited, scared to breathe. It beeped through and a woman said, "Hello?"

Her mother's voice sounded thicker, like she had a cold.

"Mum?" Kath said. "It's me."

"Who's this?"

"It's me. Katherine."

Silence on the other end. A car slithered by.

"I think you have the wrong number."

"No, Mum, it's me, Katherine."

The woman sighed. "I don't know any Katherine. You have the wrong number."

She hung up, leaving nothing but a flatline hum. The sound of death. A patient dying. But no crash team would rush in to revive her.

It was just as Matthew Hopkins had said.

Katherine Bright did not exist.

The moan began low in her throat, rising up from her breast, the low of a cow in an abattoir, and it broke out of her and keened into a long, loud howl of despair.

She climbed to her feet, pulling the knife out of the soil and thought for an instant of drawing it across her throat. To end it. End it all, this moment. End it now.

No.

She tottered, tripping as she stumbled towards the dovecote, holding out her bloody hand, and she fell right through it.

— 29 —

Her heart thumping in her throat, Kath pushed the red door open and stepped into the hallway, her way lit by a shaft of moonlight through the stained-glass panel above the front door. The stairs before her.

She was back here again to the same moment, dripping blood on Florence Cawley's hall rug.

A scuffle from upstairs. A muffled cry.

Matthew Hopkins was up there, strangling Florence. She could stop it again.

And if she did, would it end her own life? Would it mean that Kath Bright was never born? She would save Florence and go back to a world where her mother didn't recognize her.

She delved into her coat pocket, her fingers finding the plastic handle of the chef's knife, and pulled it out. It glinted silver in the moonlight.

She would do it again. Drive the knife into him again. Kill him properly this time. Even if saving Florence meant she would never be born, she could risk that.

"Stop."

She reeled. A voice behind her.

Two figures stood in the doorway, backlit by moonlight.

A man in a fedora. A woman in a bonnet.

The man stepped forward and reached out to her.

Kath held the knife up between them.

But he simply grabbed her wrist.

She felt the heat of his grip. He twisted the knife away and with his other hand smacked her on the forehead.

She had a moment only to see he had a waxed moustache, recognizing Mitch, before she fell back.

The stairs opened up and swallowed her and she plummeted into the cellar but never landed.

— 30 —

She opened her eyes. Lying on her side. Her ground floor flat with hardly any furniture. The books on the shelf in the corner alcove she'd unpacked last weekend. She was lying on her sofa in the morning light. A radio babbling *Fairytale of New York* in the flat above.

She eased herself up. She was in her maxi-dress and long coat, the paisley shawl had fallen onto the floor by the sofa. Would she have curled up on the sofa with her boots still on?

Head thumping, like she'd spent a night on the booze. But she'd drunk nothing. One of those unfair hangovers.

Had she been there or dreamed it all?

Mitch had punched her awake again. Either he had the power to knock her into the next century or he'd carried her back home.

She dug out her iPhone and hit the same number.

It rang and rang and rang. She was about to throw it across the room when her mother's voice answered.

"Hello?"

"Mum?"

A silence. An eternity in three seconds.

"Katherine? Are you all right?"

"Oh, God, Mum. You know me."

"What's up, pet?"

She was laughing.

"Are you crying, Katherine?"

"No, Mum. I'm laughing. Everything's fine."

"What's up?"

"I had a nightmare, that's all. I just needed to hear your voice."

She could hear her mother's smile through the static.

"Aw, pet, don't worry. It's only a bad dream."

She wished it were only that, and that a mother's words could make it all go away.

"How's the new job?" her Mum asked.

"I don't know yet. I'm on a probationary period but I don't think the boss likes me."

"What? Katherine! Everyone likes you."

Kath let it go. Her Mum *would* think that, but the evidence said otherwise. Darren didn't like her, Timothy didn't like her, and this Mitch who punched her in the face didn't like her.

"Well, I think he wanted someone else for my job, a friend of his, so he'd rather I fail."

"They can't do that. There's laws. You stand up to him."

"I will, Mum."

"Promise me."

"I promise."

"That's better."

"I'd better get to work. Don't want to give him a reason to sack me."

"Okay. I'll see you at Christmas?"

"Yes. It's next week. I can't wait."

She hung up and reached for her handbag, wincing at the stinging pain in her palm. She pulled out the folder of research on Florence Cawley and rifled through photocopies, wondering if any of it had changed. But no, Florence Cawley had been murdered. She had been burnt to death in her own home. And only Katherine knew that Matthew Hopkins had sneaked in quietly and strangled her in her bed first. She wondered if he'd raped her too. Or she had dreamed it all and knew nothing of what had happened on that night.

She'd failed. She'd changed nothing.

Of course she had. She was just a girl going quietly mad. A girl who'd gone home exhausted from a day and a half without sleep, a girl who'd dreamed of saving Florence Cawley, and woken hungover on her sofa.

She stuffed the folder into her bag, slung it over her shoulder and walked out, slamming the door.

She was on the bus and halfway to town, sailing through downbeat Highgate, when she noticed her fingers stained burgundy red, the scarf still wrapped tight around her hand. She dug it deep into her pocket. She could wash it when she got to work. She was going in dressed in last night's clothes, having not washed, for the second time this week. And this time with no excuse as she was coming from home, not the staff room sofa.

Trudging up New Street, with the German marketeers setting up, she thought of not going in. A child turning back before the school gates to go spend the day on the wag. She could run away, go to the cinema, have a meter-long hot dog for lunch and get drunk on *glühwein*. Sod the expense.

She'd failed to save Florence Cawley. She'd failed to prepare the exhibition. She'd be sacked. Her mother would be disappointed to discover that no one liked her. Why go in and put herself through Timothy's humiliation?

But she walked into the Central Library and let the great concrete inverted ziggurat swallow her.

— 31 —

"That's a different look for you," Liz said.

The maxi-skirt. Kath took off the long coat and hung it. She delved into the pocket and felt the plastic handle of the chef's knife. Shame faced, she folded her coat inside out and hung it so the chef's knife was hidden inside, hoping it would hang there all day and no one would see it.

She was a stupid, deluded mad woman with a knife in her coat. She would be in the nuthouse for Christmas.

"What happened to your hand?" Liz asked.

She'd washed it and taken the bloody scarf off, but there was an angry crimson gash across her palm.

"Cut it. Kitchen accident. Stupid really."

"You should get that looked at, or bandaged."

"I washed it and put antiseptic on it. It'll just have to heal now. Fresh air is best."

She settled into the morning's work, trying to gather some more material for the exhibition, but it was a couple of bricks cemented in place, when she needed to build a house by noon.

Before the big bad wolf came to blow her house down.

Mid-morning, she climbed the spiral staircase to the research room to swap shifts with Liz so she could get access to the photographic archive and at least get a few more bricks in place. There was hardly anybody in the place. Just a few Greys getting the last hours of library time before Christmas.

She caught her breath.

It was them. An old lady and a younger man in a fedora hat with a waxed moustache, sitting over an archive box.

"Liz?" she said. "Can you see them?"

"What? Those two?"

Kath checked the list of borrowed research items. *Mitchell and Hudson.*

They were there. Liz could see them.

Sweet relief flooded her. She wasn't mad. "What are they looking at?"

Liz checked the list. "Oh, that's funny. They're looking at records of Moseley Hall. What a coincidence."

Liz clumped down the spiral staircase to take over the sixth floor. Kath stared at Mitch and Mrs. Hudson. They didn't see her coming till she was standing over their table. Whispering among themselves, they became aware of her presence and looked up, caught out, sheepish.

"Is there something you need to tell me?" Kath said.

They shared a look. Mrs. Hudson slid a page of photocopied text over an illustration of the Moseley dovecote.

Kath pulled up a chair and sat opposite. "I saw you both, last night. You were there. You stopped me."

"We don't know what you mean," Mrs. Hudson

began.

Mitch clutched the old woman's hand and said, "It's time. She knows."

Mrs. Hudson shrugged, irritated.

"It really happened," Kath said. It was almost a question.

"That depends what you mean," Mrs. Hudson said.

Kath lowered her voice and leaned in closer. "I travelled to 1889 to try to prevent a murder, and you were both there."

They didn't laugh. They sat back, poker-faced.

It was true. If it wasn't true, they would be snorting derision.

"So it really happened," Kath said, almost talking to herself now. "Time travel. It's happening all the time, as if I can't hold on to the here and now. I keep..."

"Slipping," Mitch said. "It can feel like an accident at first. People talk of timeslips. I guess it makes people feel more comfortable about it."

"You mean it's not an accident?"

"No," said Mrs. Hudson. "It's you who's doing it."

"I don't have any control of this. I would stop it if I could. It's happening *to* me. I didn't ask for it."

"But you did control it," Mrs. Hudson said. "You chose to go back there last night. You chose the date. You chose the moment. It was all you."

"Yes. But not the other times. I thought I was going mad." She slumped, choked back a sob, swallowed it. She would not cry in front of these two.

Mitch let out a pained sigh, as if he felt what she was feeling. He reached out across the table.

Kath yanked her hand away.

"I'm sorry," he said. "It will get easier, I promise."

117

Mrs. Hudson tutted and folded her arms.

"We'll help you," Mitch said.

"You didn't help me last night."

"That was very necessary," Mrs. Hudson snapped. "Believe me."

Kath looked at Mitch. "You punched me in the face. Twice."

Mitch gasped. "I did not. I patted you on the shoulder. I would never punch anyone, let alone a lady."

His hand went to his heart as if she'd stabbed him.

The chef's knife was in her coat pocket downstairs.

"It might've felt like a punch to you," Mrs. Hudson said. "But he really did only give you a little nudge. Just to send you back to your own time. To here."

It had felt like a punch in the face with a sledgehammer. Both times. She had woken reeling, almost seeing stars.

"But why?" Kath said. "I was trying to save her. You stopped me. Florence Cawley is dead because of you."

"She was always dead," said Mrs. Hudson. "It always happened. You can't change that."

"If I can't change the past, why are you trying so hard to stop me doing exactly that?"

They looked at the table.

"Because I *can* change the past. I *can* save Florence Cawley, can't I?"

She *had* changed it. She could go back to that same night. She could go back whenever she chose. She could stop Matthew Hopkins, maybe even before he ever set eyes on Florence Cawley.

"I know what you're thinking," Mitch said. "But it's very important that you don't try to change the past."

"So I should just let her be murdered by that

madman." She knew there was no other way.

"We've seen some awful tragedies because people meddled with the past," said Mitch.

"What if you stopped him," said Mitch, "and in doing that, *you* died? You save her and it's the end of *you.*"

She had done exactly that: wiped out her own existence. She folded her arms and nodded.

"Oh, you *did,* didn't you?" Mitch said. "You took an axe to your family tree."

"Or a kitchen knife," Mrs Hudson said.

Kath looked at her hands on the table, knotting her fingers. She noticed her fingernails ringed red.

"There's no waking up from that," Mrs. Hudson said. "You don't wake up from it and think it was a dream. You're dead."

"Or someone else is dead. Someone else doesn't exist because you meddled with the past."

"We've seen it happen."

Florence Cawley was dead, murdered by that madman, and she always would be. Even though Kath had the power to go back and stop it happening, she would never be allowed to. Matthew Hopkins would always get away with it. It seemed so wrong.

Mitch patted her hand again, as if he'd heard her thought. "Don't worry. He got what he deserved."

"He bloody did not. He didn't hang."

"He was insane."

Slobbering in a padded cell. Kath shivered at the thought. A living hell.

"You have all this power and you can't do anything with it," she said. "It's all for nothing. And here I am, about to be sacked because I wasted all this time." She laughed. "It's funny, the idea of wasting time, when I'm a bloody time traveller."

"What do you mean, you're about to be sacked?" Mrs. Hudson asked.

"I've just started work here. I'm on probation. I neglected the exhibition I was supposed to be preparing because of…" she waved her arm in the air, as if to indicate Florence Cawley's murder. All of it. Everything. "My boss is going to come in an hour from now and ask to see all the things I've prepared, and I have nothing. Well, almost nothing."

Mrs Hudson looked at Mitch. Kath sensed them agree on something.

"How long will it take you to prepare what you need?" Mrs Hudson asked.

Kath looked at her watch, as if she'd find the time there. "It's a full day's work, if I really go at it. And I mean a full day, working into the night. I just don't have the time."

"We can help you," Mitch said.

"That's nice, but you can't do anything in an hour."

"No, we can't," Mrs. Hudson said, and she smiled for the first time. "But we have more than an hour. We have all the time in the world."

— 32 —

The first thing they did was walk out.

"We're going to need supplies," Mitch said, "if we're pulling an all-nighter."

Kath sat for half an hour waiting for them to come back, wondering if this was all a joke. The research room was empty now. The Greys had all packed up and gone home for Christmas. Kath laid out her research for the exhibition. A neat collection of photocopies indicating the pictures and paintings that would feature, with her scribbled text accompanying. It was about a quarter of what was needed.

Just thirty minutes till her meeting with Timothy.

Mrs Hudson came back with clingfilm-wrapped cheese and pickle sandwiches, bags of ready salted crisps and red apples. Probably the same meal deal Kath had got in the newsagents at the top of New Street. Mitch came back with a stainless-steel thermos flask, a big one, in a British Home Stores carrier bag.

"I took it to the Starbucks on New Street and asked them to fill it up."

"This should see us through," Mrs. Hudson said.

"What exactly are we going to do?" Kath asked,

checking her wristwatch.

"Where do we need to do the work, my dear?"

"Through there, in the photographic archive, and in here."

"Can you think of a time recently when the place was empty and you know no one was here?"

Kath thought hard about the last week. "I suppose night time is best. You can work here all night and the security staff don't come in and disturb you. I did it Wednesday night."

"We can't do it that night," said Mitch. "You don't want to disturb yourself."

Kath realized what they were planning. "Tuesday night. No one was here then."

"Tuesday night it is, then," said Mrs. Hudson. "Get everything you need to take with you."

Kath went down the spiral staircase where Liz was sitting doing nothing, texting on her phone under the reception counter. A couple of Greys were left, researching to the bitter end. She reached for her coat and handbag.

Liz nodded as if she understood. Kath muttered something about it being cold up there.

She scooted back up the spiral staircase and put all her research into her folder. The exhibition folder, not the Florence Cawley folder. She left that behind. It was time to do the work she was supposed to do.

Mitch and Mrs. Hudson stood in the middle of the research room, coats and scarves on, holding their bags; an old lady and her young fogey son, waiting for the coach to take them on a day trip.

They formed a séance circle, holding hands awkwardly, the bags and folders tucked under their arms. Mrs. Hudson began intoning a low chant.

"Tuesday the sixteenth of December, 2008. 7pm… Tuesday the sixteenth of December, 2008. 7pm… Tuesday the sixteenth of December, 2008. 7pm…"

The room shifted. Something about the light, or perhaps the air had flipped in on itself. Kath wondered if it was the atmospheric pressure of three people suddenly appearing and pushing out the air. Her ears popped and she felt a buzz of electricity pass through her.

"We're here," Mrs. Hudson said.

It was hard to tell that anything had changed. No. The high windows, just a slit above the bookshelves. They were black. It was night. And rain was drumming on them. It had rained that night.

Someone walking downstairs.

They looked down the spiral staircase and saw Kath walk past, wrapping her scarf around her neck.

Kath stared in blank horror at seeing herself outside herself for the first time. She remembered she'd just discovered that Florence Cawley was her ancestor and everything seemed right and logical with the world. She'd worked till seven and walked through town in the rain to go to bed early with a hot water bottle. She remembered the giddiness of that sound sleep. So long ago. Only three days.

"That was you," Mrs Hudson said.

"Yes... I worked until seven."

"That was close. You don't want to meet yourself now. We should have made it half past."

Mitch put the thermos flask on the desk.

Mrs. Hudson dumped her carrier bag down and took off her coat. "Right. Let's do it."

Kath showed them the photographic archive and how

to pull up the right resources. She gave them the list of a hundred references she had and they set off to gather them. As they pulled them up and deposited them on the giant square desk, Kath made photocopies and wrote an explanatory note on each one. The exhibition began to take shape. As they worked through the night, she sketched a map, plotting a journey, a story that the public could follow.

They stopped for coffee and sandwiches at about midnight. She worked out that it would be 5pm back in her own a time, on Friday. The staff party would be over and Kath would be sacked and heading home for Christmas. But actually it wouldn't be that at all. They would go back to 11.30, the exact same moment from which they had departed, and it would all have taken no more than a few seconds. In a way, they had stepped outside time.

At one in the morning, she went through to look for a pencil sketch portrait of Joseph Priestley that had been misfiled, and shuddered at the thought of the door to Mason College appearing again. A secret door to another time.

What would those night watchmen have done to her if they'd caught her? If Mitch hadn't been waiting there to send her back.

She walked through the cavernous space of the stacks, her heels echoing. Turning into that aisle. The door wasn't there.

She heaved a sigh of relief and turned away. And then there was a noise behind her, An implosion.

She looked back.

The door wasn't there.

Florence Cawley was there.

Kath jerked back in fright.

Had she come back to ask why Kath had let her die?

The woman let out an *oh* of surprise and then grinned.

It wasn't Florence Cawley. It was herself. It was Katherine.

Her double held up a palm in apology. "Don't be scared. I've come to help."

Kath stared at herself. This was nothing like looking at oneself in a mirror. This image of herself breathed and moved to her own heartbeat.

"The film you need for the exhibition. The gymkhana tournament."

"It's not in the Huntley Archive," Kath said.

"I know. He hid it, to sabotage you."

"Bastard."

Her doppelganger smirked. "Don't worry, you'll get him back for it. Look in Winson Green Lunatic Asylum archives. His little joke."

"Thank you," Kath said.

"Don't tell Mrs Hudson and Mitch I did this."

"Why not?"

"Oh, and make the most of this Christmas with Mum. Every bit of it."

A door opened and echoed through the great space of the archives. Mitch was heading for her.

Kath glanced back but her double was gone.

Mitch came for her, his brogues echoing.

She hurried to the Winson Green Asylum archives. A shelf of old cardboard boxes stuffed with case files from a hundred years ago. Sitting on top of one, a little box that looked out of place. A neat label, handwritten, *Moseley Hall Homemade Film. Huntley Archive 17895.*

She grabbed it and turned as Mitch arrived.

"What's wrong?" he said. "You look like you've seen a ghost."

"I did. I think. God, that was weird."

"What did you see?"

"Myself."

"Oh," he said. "But you've gone home. We saw you leave."

"It wasn't me from Monday night."

"What?"

"I think it was me from the future."

"Did your future self tell you anything?"

"No," Kath lied. "Just smiled and then she was gone. It was only a couple of seconds."

"Right," Mitch said. "Don't tell Mrs Hudson, all right? She'll only worry."

Kath nodded and swallowed a ball of guilt.

They pushed on through the night, and she was surprised to find it was all finished in three hours. She found herself crying for no reason: she was so tired.

She had met herself. There were no ghosts, only the experience of time. She had met herself from the future. There had been something in the look, something in the smile, as if her future self knew so much more. That older self had looked on her with pity, like she was seeing herself as a child, so innocent, before she'd become an adult.

Her Mum was going to die. This would be their last Christmas together. She had all but said it.

Kath shuddered and cringed the memory away. It was no good thinking about how Future Kath might come and tell her things. It would drive you mad.

Mrs. Hudson looked at her watch with a satisfied

smile. "We did that in good time."

"I need a good sleep," said Mitch. "Or it's another Christmas with the flu for me."

Kath drew all the paperwork together and stacked it, sliding it into the folder. It was done. She had everything Timothy needed.

They put on their coats, formed a circle, and in moments they were back at 11.31 on Friday.

— 33 —

They stretched and yawned, three people at the end of a long shift.

"And it's not even lunchtime yet," Mitch joked.

Kath couldn't believe that only a minute had passed. Grey afternoon light at the windows. No rain. They had stolen a day. She giggled at the thought of never having to miss another deadline again.

Mitch seemed to read her thought. "Don't do this too often. It gets very tiring. Wipes you out."

That was why he always seemed to have the flu.

"Before we go," Mrs. Hudson said, "we should swap numbers, to keep in touch."

Kath took out her mobile and keyed in their numbers. Two new contacts, the strangest she had ever gathered.

"Well, Merry Christmas, I suppose," Mitch said.

"Thank you both. But…"

"What is it?" Mrs. Hudson asked.

"Can I just ask… Why? Why have you helped me like this?"

"Because you're with us now," Mitch said. "You're part of our team. We help each other."

A team. A secret cabal of time cops. She was part of that now. She couldn't help feeling thrilled.

"Besides, this place is very useful," Mrs. Hudson said, "You need to keep this job."

She was joking, but only half joking.

"I saw you," Kath said. "Before this all began."

"Oh, really?" Mrs Hudson said.

"I thought it was a dream, but I really don't think it was now. I think it was the first time I did this… thing. I was running through the square, past the Town Hall. Not the time Mitch stopped me. Earlier than that. It was different. There were hovels all around. Snow. A poster advertising a reading by Charles Dickens at the Town Hall. You called out to me. I saw you before I knew you."

Again that look passing between them.

"I don't think that's happened to me yet," Mrs Hudson said.

"Write it down," said Mitch. "Every little detail. It might be useful."

The old woman pulled her in and gave her a hug with a strength that took her breath away. Mitch stepped forward and shook her hand, giving a little nod, stopping just short of clicking his heels.

She followed them down the spiral staircase, the three of them winding their way down, clomping round and round in circles.

Liz looked up with surprise. "Oh, I thought we were empty. You're the very last ones. We're closing now."

"Yes, we know," Mrs. Hudson beamed. "Do have a jolly old Christmas."

Kath noticed Mrs Hudson was putting on a sweet old lady's voice. There was nothing of the steely resolve she'd shown before. They tottered off and glided away down the escalator, and Kath felt a sudden pang of loss. Would she really not see them till after Christmas?

She realized how much she wanted to belong to something. She wasn't such a lone wolf after all.

Liz came to her side. "Thank God the Greys have buggered off. It's holiday time."

Timothy came out of the staff room. "Oh there you are, Kath. Time for our meeting."

Kath beamed the brightest, most confident smile she'd felt crack her face in months. She held up the folder bulging with content, and the little cardboard box of film. "Yes, it's all here."

She caught his look of surprise.

Liz whispered *good luck* as she went through.

— Epilogue —

"I must say I'm surprised," Timothy said. He sat back in his chair, nodding. "This is very thorough, meticulously researched."

"Thank you," she said.

"I can't believe you've done it with so little time."

"There were a few late nights involved. Three, in fact."

He nodded again and closed the folder, rapped it with his knuckles. "Well, you certainly earned your Christmas break."

"Does that mean I'm coming back after the holiday?"

Timothy smiled through gritted teeth. "Let's put our little disagreement behind us."

A wave of fatigue hit her as she walked back out to the sixth floor, where Liz was putting on her coat.

"You not staying for the party?" said Kath.

"Oh yes. I'll go through that," Liz said. "But I'm running right out of the door as soon as I can."

Kath packed her own things. She left her bulging research folder there, where it would stay over the holiday, and hid the box of film away so Timothy couldn't hide it again. She didn't need to think about any of it over Christmas. There was too much going on.

She wondered if she'd meet with Mrs Hudson and Mitch. There was so much to talk about. How she might control this thing, this miracle. Time travel. It was too weird.

She yawned as they took the lift down to the ground floor. It was only 12.30 but she'd been working for twelve, no, thirteen hours.

The library was shutting down and all staff gathering in the ground floor Children's Library. An iPod speaker played Christmas swing tunes and a buffet was laid out.

Liz went straight for the wine and necked it with relief.

It seemed like everyone wanted to go home for the holidays, or to get that Christmas shopping, or on to a better party, with real friends. There were infinitely better things to do than stand around in a children's library eating soggy sausage rolls with people you barely knew.

Timothy took her arm and insisted on introducing her to some boring suit. "This is Katherine Bright," he brayed. "She really is the bright new star of Local Studies."

He guffawed at his own joke and Kath felt the wine curdle on her tongue. This was the man who'd tried to sack her for Christmas, now showing her off as his best new team member.

She managed to pull away. Liz beckoned her over.

"I just wanted to say something before I go."

"I'll see you after Christmas."

"Yes, but I wanted to say, well done. You beat him."

"I don't understand," Kath said. "What was that?"

"Timothy might want his friend in your job, but he

still has to impress the big boss. And you've just pulled off the impossible."

She chinked her glass and Kath felt a surge of euphoria sweep through her to crackle around her skull like a static charge.

Liz left after an hour, singing, "Merry Christmas. I'm off to sunny Dartmoor!"

Kath couldn't shake off the feeling that she would never see her again. She stayed half an hour longer. Enough people had slipped away that it didn't look bad.

She walked out through Chamberlain Square and couldn't help looking back up at the concrete inverted ziggurat, almost expecting to see the gothic facade of Mason College instead.

She pushed through the German market and stopped at a TV window display. The news was reporting Woolworth's had gone bankrupt, announcing 807 UK stores would close. 27,000 people out of work just in time for Christmas. The MFI furniture store had ceased trading too. 111 stores closed. 1,400 people redundant. These were stores that had been there her whole life, and most of her parents' lives too. A tornado was wreaking destruction across the land.

She got the 50 home, nodding off a couple of times as the bus trundled through Highgate and Balsall Heath. As it reached Moseley village, she got up and stepped off two stops early.

She resisted the urge to walk up that side street and see the house round the corner; the house where Florence Cawley had been murdered a century ago. Last night.

Instead, she turned and faced the squat tower across the road, busy with traffic.

The dovecote.

She crossed and stood with her hands on the wooden fence, longing to climb over and go touch it. Too many people around. Cars and buses rushing past. People waiting at the bus stop right there.

But she gazed on it. Just an old brick tower in a garden on the edge of a suburban hospital site. It hummed and resonated with that same power, deeper now, vibrating in her breastbone. She held it inside and knew it for what it was now.

It was a power for her, and her alone.

Thank you

… for buying and reading *The Ghosts of Paradise Place*

If you liked it, please take a minute or two to give it a short review where you bought it. You won't be seeing adverts for Touchstone books on billboards or station platforms, but a simple review can really make a difference to an independent author like me. They help to promote my books and that helps me put out even more.

Also by Andy Conway

Crossing over into the Touchstone world, and linking with
The Ghosts of Paradise Place, this horror story deals with Liz,
Sian and Zara's Christmas trip to a remote cottage on
Dartmoor to escape problems at home. Haunted by the dark
history of witchfinders and ancient superstitions, their long
hike across the moor turns tragic as old ghosts return for
vengeance…

*"Dartmoor at Christmastime. What a spine-tinglingly perfect
setting for a ghost story… It might arguably be described as a
present-day M.R. James, as thoroughly malevolent ghosts wreak
havoc on our heroines… It's a cracking little ghost story."*

Available in eBook

FREE DOWNLOAD

**A chilling investigation into the truth
behind the Touchstone series...**

"A cracking, spooky short story which is a real head-wrecker..."

Jack Turner, author *Valentine's Day*

Sign up for Andy Conway's New Releases mailing list at
andyconway.net to get a free copy of
The Reluctant Time Traveller.

Acknowledgements

A big thank you to Prudence S. Thomas, whose research into Britain's witch trials provided valuable background to this tale. Prudence writes a series of fantasy novels set in a fictional version of Lancashire, taking inspiration from the Forest of Bowland, Lancaster Castle and the famous witch trials.

David Wake is a brilliant editor who pushed me to make this so much better than my initial effort.

My Touchstone Launch Team — Paul Gray, Lee Sharp, Audrey Finta, Helena George and Lorna Rose — all made sure the book was a much more satisfying read, made sense and was free of errors, although I would stress that any remaining errors, especially historical errors, are all down to me, and me alone.

Historical Notes

Moseley Dovecote. Part of the Moseley Hall estate, the dovecote is an 18th century octagonal brick dovecote and adjoining cowhouse, now housing a permanent exhibition about dovecotes and temporary exhibitions of local interest.

German market. The Frankfurt Christmas Market and Craft Market is an annual outdoor Christmas market and craft fair which has been held in Birmingham since 2001. Birmingham is twinned with Frankfurt, and the market is affiliated with the Frankfurt Christmas Market.

Iron:Man is a statue by Antony Gormley, in Victoria Square, Birmingham, England. Six metres (20 ft) tall, it is said by the sculptor to represent the traditional skills of Birmingham and the Black Country practised during the Industrial Revolution. The statue was moved into storage on 5 September 2017, to allow the tracks for the Midlands Metro extension to Centenary Square to be laid.

Floozie in the Jacuzzi. *The River*, locally known as the *Floozie in the Jacuzzi*, is an artwork in Victoria

Square. On either side of the fountain are two large sculptures collectively known as *Guardians.* The sculptures are not identical and take features from a variety of animals, so they aren't in reality gryphons.

Chamberlain Square was drastically remodelled in the 1970s, with most of the Victorian buildings demolished, and the John Madin-designed brutalist Central Library (also now demolished) overpowering the square. The square is once again under development as part of the Paradise scheme.

Birmingham Central Library was the main public library in Birmingham from 1974 until 2013. For a time the largest non-national library in Europe. Designed by architect John Madin in the brutalist style, the library gained architectural praise as an icon of British brutalism with its stark use of concrete, bold geometry, inverted ziggurat sculptural form and monumental scale. The building was demolished in 2016.

World Cup 1966, Villa Park. This photograph references the Touchstone book, *All the Time in the World.* The mysterious man in the photograph Kath recognizes, is, of course, Danny Pearce.

Sally's Oak. This is indeed a myth with no historical foundation, although the name was actually recorded as *Sally Oak* on a canal map produced by John Snape in 1789.

Edmund Meckle is a fictional character who appears in Andy Conway's short story *Ghosts on the Moor.* The story deals with Liz and her friends' Christmas trip to Dartmoor and the tragic events that ensue.

Mason Science College was founded in 1875 by industrialist and philanthropist Sir Josiah Mason. Paul Cadbury referred to it in 1952 as 'a neo-gothic monstrosity.' It was demolished in 1964, along with the original Central Public Library (which features in the Touchstone book, *Bright Star Rising*). Birmingham Central Library stood on the site of the old college.

Dark 'mob' scandal that shames our city. This fictional news story is from the finale of the Touchstone book, *All the Time in the World*.

Lakota history. This, of course, looks forward to Kath's adventures in the Touchstone books, *Bright Star Falling* and *Bright Star Rising*.

Penguin edition. A vision of Kath buying this book as a girl appears in *Bright Star Falling*. A remarkable book in the Ladybird children's history series, *Battle of the Little Big Horn: Custer's Last Stand* (General Interest, Series 707) by Frank Humphris (Ladybird Books Ltd, 1976) presents an admirably progressive view of Lakota culture and their fight for survival.

Matthew Hopkins and Florence Cawley. This murder case is an entirely fictional invention, but there was a late-Victorian 'witch' murder case in the Midlands from 14 years earlier. The Warwickshire Advertiser of September 1875 records the murder of 80-year-old Ann Tennant of Long Compton by labourer John Hayward, who believed she was a witch who had caused harm to his farm animals.

Detective Inspector Beadle is a fictional detective who appears in several Touchstone books: *The Sins of the Fathers, Buried in Time* and *Bright Star Rising*.

Steelhouse Lane Police Station. The police station was built in 1933 and closed its doors in 2017. The adjacent, late-nineteenth century cellblock on the corner of Coleridge Passage was in use from 1891 to 2016 and many of the original Victorian features are still present.

It currently offers events and tours. See Andy Conway's YouTube channel for footage of its open day.

Versailles timeslip. The Moberly–Jourdain incident is a claim of time travel and hauntings made by Charlotte Anne Moberly and Eleanor Jourdain. In 1911, Moberly and Jourdain published a book entitled *An Adventure* under the names of Elizabeth Morison and Frances Lamont, describing a visit to the Palace of Versailles where they claimed to have seen the gardens as they had been in the late eighteenth century, as well as Marie Antoinette.

Clava Cairns timeslip. This incident, and the Versailles timeslip, are featured in the Marshall Cavendish partwork, *The Unexplained* (page 648), which the author collected every week as a schoolboy in 1977. These timeslip stories were the earliest inspirations for the Touchstone series.

Liverpool Bold Street timeslip. This story, featuring an ex-policeman named 'Frank', is featured widely across the Internet but is difficult to pin down to a reliable source. RationalWiki's Time Slip entry mentions it.

Mrs Hudson is, of course, a major character in the Touchstone books.

Charles Dickens reading. Dickens did, indeed, perform the first ever public reading of *A Christmas Carol* at Birmingham Town Hall in 1844.

Paradise Forum was the name given to the shopping arcade created under Central Library in the early 1990s. When the library's atrium was enclosed with a glass roof and screens in 1991, the space below was named Paradise Forum.

Christ Church dominated what was then City Council Square (now Victoria Square) in Birmingham, roughly taking up the entire plot of what is now the home of the 'Floozie in the Jacuzzi'. It stood from 1805 to 1899. It features in *Buried in Time*, and also in *Bright Star Rising*.

Council House Square. Now Victoria Square, and very different in character in 1889. While the Council House and the Town Hall remain, the old square was dominated by Christ Church. There are tantalising glimpses of what this square looked like in several photographs from the late 1800s. There is also an illustration from 1886 by H. W. Brewer, taken from *The Graphic* which gives a bird's eye view of the city centre. I have posted these images on the Touchstone Pinterest site.

Statues of city elders looking down. Kath is confusing these statues. Council House Square contained statues of John Skirrow Wright, Joseph Priestley and Robert Peel. Only Priestley's statue was moved to Chamberlain Square.

Paradise Place existed as a place name for part of the concrete warren of John Madin's Brutalist complex. The most ironic use of the word 'paradise' ever. The name is still used to refer to the general area incorporating Chamberlain Square and its surroundings.

Paradise Street is a short street in Birmingham City Centre and runs roughly from Victoria Square to Suffolk Street and Broad Street. The street has existed since 1796. It is noted as the location of Birmingham Town Hall. The street gave its name to Paradise Circus, which lies adjacent.

Chamberlain Square timelapse film. In the 1960s and 70s research chemist and amateur photographer Derek Fairbrother made over 20 photographic time-lapse sequences showing the demolition of old buildings and their replacement by new buildings and road systems in Birmingham city centre. His photographs of the building of Birmingham Central Library were exhibited as a film in the exhibition *Birmingham Seen* at Gas Hall in 2010. The film can be seen on Andy Conway's Touchstone Pinterest site.

Mitch has been an ever-present character throughout the Touchstone saga. Here, for the first time, it is revealed that Mitch is a nickname derived from his surname. His first name is revealed in the Touchstone books, *Haunted Town* and *Unfinished Sympathy.*

St. Agnes church. In the first Touchstone book, *The Sins of the Fathers*, Arabella Palmer, takes the exact same journey as Kath does in Chapter 15, and also mistakes St Agnes church for St Mary's.

Sergeant Varley is a fictional police officer who might be a distant relative of Chief Superintendent Xavier Varley from the 1887-set Touchstone book, *Bright Star Rising.*

Corbett's Temperance Hotel was demolished in 1889 to make the new Birmingham post office building, which, amazingly, with the city's penchant for destroying any building made before the war, still stands. The hotel features in *Bright Star Rising.*

Pinfold Street is the location of a key scene in the Touchstone book, *Buried in Time.* It also features in *Bright Star Rising.*

Released next in the Touchstone saga

Unfinished Sympathy [Touchstone Season 2]
(Released: August 22nd, 2019)
Searching for his long lost love, Mitch finds himself in New
York, 1908, and caught up in a blackmail plot with world
famous composer Gustav Mahler and his wife Alma.
A gripping tale of murder, blackmail, adultery and scandal set
in the last days of New York's Gilded Age.

Make sure you're the first in line to read it by joining Andy
Conway's Touchstone mailing list at andyconway.net

Also by Andy Conway

Touchstone Season 1

Over the course of six novels, and an entire century of local history, **Touchstone Season 1** builds into a moving coming-of-age saga that has won plaudits from young and old readers alike with its intelligent blend of time travel adventure, science fiction, historical romance and fantasy.

"I believe it's one of the best series of its kind."

"Had me hooked from start to finish... It's a magnificent story."

"If you haven't read this series yet — you simply must! But beware — you will be hooked!"

"Only surpassed by Jack Finney the master in time travel, but if this guy carries on in same vein I cannot wait."

Available in paperback editions and eBook box set collection

Buried in Time *Touchstone Season 2].* The Touchstone series of time travel historical adventures continues with this stand-alone opener to the second season, a Victorian suspense thriller dripping with mystery and horror.

July, 1888. Two months before Jack the Ripper's Whitechapel murders begin, a killer stalks the streets of Victorian Birmingham, the heart of England's industrial revolution.

Are the clues to his horrific crimes in a series of macabre paintings by Daniel Pearce, an artist suffering amnesia and desperately trying to uncover his lost past before his impending marriage?

Arthur Conan Doyle, Catherine Eddowes and Tom Conway, a mysterious time-travelling writer, stalk this gripping and bloody Victorian crime novel that explores the real identity of Jack the Ripper, only weeks before he set out for London, to carve his name into history. Can Daniel Pearce stop the Ripper before he starts, or are his actions creating the world's first serial killer?

"Inventively brilliant alternative history... deeper, darker and more inventive."

"Great read, and thought provoking on whom Jack the Ripper really was."

Available in eBook and paperback

Bright Star Falling *[Touchstone Season 2].* The time travel saga goes into the West... When a mysterious redhead plunges from the sky onto the Montana plains in 1874, she is taken in by Sitting Bull's tribe and named Bright Star Falling. Torn between dark dreams of the past and bloody visions of the future, might she be the spirit whose re-appearance spells the end of the Lakota people? *Bright Star Falling* is an epic journey through the old West, a sweeping historical fantasy of life on the plains, and one woman's desperate, bloody struggle to find a way home.

"I have been waiting for the release of the eighth novel in the Touchstone series and this fabulous book definitely did not disappoint. A brilliant and enjoyable read, I couldn't put it down!"

"Fantastic story. A world away from the Birmingham of season one but the Wild West and time travel what a brilliant combination."

"We had to wait a while for the next instalment in the Touchstone series. But it was well worth waiting for."

Available in eBook and paperback

Bright Star Rising [Touchstone Season 2]. 1887. Buffalo Bill's Wild West show comes to Birmingham, and with it, Katherine Bright, the mysterious white woman who lived with the Lakota Native Americans for a decade. A woman with a lost past and dark magic. Escaping the show, she makes her way across the city to the mysterious dovecote of her visions: the key to her lost identity and perhaps the gateway to her forgotten life. But the city's lawless police force, a zealous Pinkerton agent, and Birmingham's notorious cutthroat gang, the Peaky Blinders, will stop at nothing to claim the price on her head.

"Touchstone saga at its best. Absolutely brilliant and highly recommended."

"Another brilliant book in the Touchstone series. The story twists and turns, with so much detail and strong links to Birmingham in another time."

Available in eBook and paperback

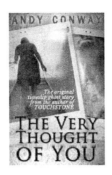

Crossing over into the Touchstone universe (specifically *Touchstone 5: Let's Fall in Love for the Last Time*), this timeslip ghost story is a moving, evocative meditation on love and betrayal and the persistence of memory.

The Very Thought of You is a novella about a young man's obsession with Amy, the dead wife of an old man he visits. Community visitor Jez is assigned Harold, a cantankerous old codger who takes a venomous delight in confrontation and lives in a house that is falling down around him. But when Jez starts to see Amy's ghost and finds himself propelled into the house's secret past, his obsession with her threatens his hold on the present.

"Suspense, mystery, intrigue and supernatural… this delivers on all aspects… Couldn't put it down! Finished it in almost one sitting."

Available in eBook

Printed in Great Britain
by Amazon

10583553R00098